Linda Porter
09

TORN BETWEEN 2 BROTHAS

LINDA PORTER

Bloomington, IN Milton Keynes, UK

authorHOUSE®

AuthorHouse™
1663 Liberty Drive, Suite 200
Bloomington, IN 47403
www.authorhouse.com
Phone: 1-800-839-8640

AuthorHouse™ UK Ltd.
500 Avebury Boulevard
Central Milton Keynes, MK9 2BE
www.authorhouse.co.uk
Phone: 08001974150

First published by AuthorHouse 1/3/2008

ISBN: 978-1-4259-8121-1 (sc)

Library of Congress Control Number: 2006910333

*Printed in the United States of America
Bloomington, Indiana*

This book is printed on acid-free paper.

This book is dedicated to my parents:
Rudolph and Roberta Ann Porter.

"We've all loved before. We've all loved so deeply that the core of our being felt as if it were drowning in an abyss of pandemonium. One day Love is wonderful and blissful…it warms your soul like a bowl of hot, buttery grits on a cold winter day and just like that…Pain will introduce himself…Pain will stab you and instead of just wounding your heart and pulling away…Pain stays and makes himself comfortable by lingering and withering to the depths of your soul…and when only an ounce of your soul is left…Love creeps around the corner and wraps the essence of her being around you like a warm blanket." LP

BROTHER #1

Okay, where do I start? Let's start with brother number one. I loved him more than a cold glass of Sparklettes water on a day when it's a 115 degrees in Las Vegas. I loved him more than collard greens, ham hocks, smothered chicken and hot-water cornbread after Sunday church services. I loved him more than a hot fudge sundae with extra syrup during that time of the month. And what did he do? He fucked up! Yes, that's what I said. He fucked up, plain and simple. When your significant other breaks your heart and you're giving someone the low down, do you say, "Oh, I caught my man with another woman, I guess he just messed up." No, for some reason no other adjective can quite take the place of the word fuck. I'm just telling it like it is.

BROTHER #2

Now, on to my current beau. I love him more than a *Chili's Top Shelf Margarita* at the end of a dreadful week, after dealing with psycho, schizo, rude, insecure, ignorant co-workers and bosses who smile in your face while stabbing you in the back. I love him more than a pedicure after wearing three-inch heels all day just to look sexy and ladylike. I love him more than great sex. You know the kind that makes you lose your breath and lay back and say, "Damn, he actually took the time to lick and touch my clit, soft and slow and didn't treat it like a miniature power tool." Simply put: I'm in love.

CHAPTER 1

Finally, I have someone who loves, respects and cherishes me for me. As Salt-N-Pepa would say, "I gotta good man!" It took some time, but he's here and I'm happy as hell and loving life. Now something told me that things have been going too smooth, for too long. Guess who pops up in the midst of my current bliss? Brotha number one. Professing his undying love for me and how sorry he is for ever hurting me. What am I supposed to do? Do I tell brotha number one to go to hell and to leave the past in the past? Do I give him another chance and end my loving relationship? Or do I just date them both? What? Why are you looking so shocked? Brothas do it all of the time. Why can't I?

CHAPTER 2

I'm a producer/fill-in-reporter in the newsroom of the NBC affiliate here in Las Vegas. During the day, I work as a sales manager at Saks Fifth Avenue in the women's clothing department. Basically, I put up with crap all day. Crap from fat women trying to squeeze their behinds into lycra and stuck up, egotistical news persons who believe the sun rises and sets on their behinds. It's a trip, but someone has to put up with it. Most of the people in the newsroom think highly of me, especially the men, and say that I'm well on my way to being a top reporter at this station. I just have to work my butt off and stay hungry. I do both because I truly believe it's my destiny to be behind the news desk. The women here are just the opposite of the men. They are so busy looking at what I have on and gawking and by to-die-for-body that they can't concentrate on doing their stories. I know that my last statement sounds conceited, I'm not. However, I do realize that I've been blessed with brains and good looks.

Don't hate me, I didn't have a damn thing to do with it. Blame my mom and dad. God rest their souls.

Anyway, the 11 o'clock news has just ended and I'm getting my things together to leave. I stuff all of my paperwork into my Dooney briefcase and head out the door. As I'm walking to car I hear a deep voice say, "Please don't leave me." I stop dead in my tracks and turn around. Before my very eyes is this fine, bronze specimen of a man named Miles Grey. Miles is one of the cameramen here at Channel 3. We've spoken a few times, but never a personal conversation. I've noticed him checking me out. Shoot, to be perfectly honest, I've been checking this African king out since day one, but he'd never know it.

"What did you say?"

"I said, 'Please don't leave me,'" he says in a smooth soft tone.

"Why?" I say with a slight edge.

"Because I want to talk to you," he says still being kind.

"About what?" I say while trying to act as if I'm not interested.

"About you."

"What about me?" I say while edging myself slightly closer.

"Everything!" he smiles. "I want to know all about you. What you like, dislike, what makes you happy, what turns you on. Everything."

"And why may I ask do you need to know these things?"

"Well, if I'm going to be a part of your life, I need to know these things."

Ain't that a blip? A part of my life? Who does this brotha thinks he is?

"A part of my life? Aren't you being a bit presumptuous?"

"No, I don't think so." He closes the space between us. "I like what I see and I'm interested in getting to know you. Why should I beat around the bush?" *He's looking at me as if he can see through me. Stop it!*

"Listen Mr. Grey," I say.

He puts a finger up to my lips. "Miles, please."

"Listen Miles, it's been a long day. I'm tired and I really don't have time for games. Have a good evening." I walk quickly to my car.

"Natalie, don't leave. Just have one cup of coffee with me and we'll call it a night. I just want to talk to you. Do I have to beg? I will if I have to."

I turn around and he's on his knees. *What the hell is Miles doing? I don't have time for this chivalry bull.*

"What are you doing?"

"I'm begging."

"Okay, but just one cup. Okay?"

"Deal."

He's smiling that wonderful smile at me again and looking at me with those eyes. I can't stand this.

"Just give me one sec to put my gear away and then we'll be on our way."

My mind is spinning. *Natalie, what the hell are you doing? Why'd you say yes? Are you crazy? Damn it!!*

I wait for him to put his camera gear away and insist that we take separate cars. We arrive at Starbuck's at the same time. He jumps out of his Jeep, runs to my car and opens the door for me. Manners. I'm impressed. We order two mocha lattes, he pulls a chair out for me to sit and then sits across from me. Home training. Two points.

I'm looking at him closely now, really checking him out. He's not drop dead gorgeous, but rather handsome and obviously very charming. He has a beautiful voice, the kind of voice that you can listen to all night. Clean cut, even in shorts and a T-shirt. Strong, large, masculine hands with manicured nails. Tall, around 6'2, 200 pounds. Not skinny, not thick, just right. Sort of a cross between a basketball and football players body. And my God; look at those feet, at least a size 12. My mind is wandering now, this brother has got to have a big dick or he has just messed up all of my imagination. *Natalie get your mind out of the gutter. I can't help it. I haven't been laid in two years. It's dryer than the Mojave Desert down there.* I almost burst out laughing to myself.

"What are you thinking about?" he says.

"Oh nothing, just trying to mentally wind down after a hard day." *Good one Natalie.*

He's staring at me again.

"Why are you looking at me like that?"

"Like what?" he says coyly.

"Like that."

"I like looking at you, you're beautiful. A little snobbish, but that's ok. It's just your security blanket. I know that you're really a sweet person."

"You think so huh?"

"Yeah," he says with a slight smile.

"And how may I ask do you think you know these things?"

"I've been observing you for a few months now, watching how you work and how you interact with others, you're sharp. And like I said, there's an arrogance, but it's not offensive, with you it's rather sexy."

"I don't know if I should be flattered or pissed off."

"Please, take it as a compliment, that's how it's meant."

"Well, thank you for the compliment," I say slightly flattered at his observations.

He smiles and licks his beautiful thick lips.

I'm gonna die. Stay cool Natalie, no man has ever affected you like this on the first date. But this isn't a date, is it?

Re-crossing my legs and taking a sip of my latte I say, "So Miles, you got me here. Now what?"

"Tell me about you."

"Like what?"

"Anything that you'd like me to know."

"I wouldn't like for you to know anything."

"Okay, I'll just sit here and look at you all evening. That suits me just fine."

He leans his chair back against the wall, puts his hands behind his head and just stares at me as if he's taking in every inch of me, noticing every detail. *I can't take much more of this.*

"Alright, let's get this over with." I realize that I'm being rude, but I can't help it. Men treat you like shit when you're nice, and I can't afford to let my guard down. I've had enough pain in my life.

"Hold up!" He leans forward. "Is this really a chore for you to sit down and engage in some friendly conversation? If so, you're welcome to leave…because I wouldn't want to ruin your evening." He's slightly pissed, slightly hurt and even looks a little sad.

Now what Nat?

"Miles, I'm sorry. I know that you're trying to be nice to me, but…"

"But what? You've been hurt before, you don't have time for games, you don't trust men?"

"So you're a mind reader now?"

"No, I can just sense your pain. Look at how uneasy it is for you to just sit here and talk. I'm not going to bite you. At least not hard!"

We both laugh.

"Miles, you are a trip."

"Around the world, if you let me take you." He takes my hand in his and kisses it softly. He's flirting and I like it. We wind up being the last people to leave Starbuck's. I don't know where the time went, but it seemed to fly. We talked about our lives and past relationships. Both of us had been hurt very badly and are trying to put the pain behind us. He seemed to be doing a good job. His job at the station occupies most of his time and he really loves what he does. Miles has hopes of becoming a filmmaker one day, our next Spike Lee.

Miles walks me to my car and we decide to stand outside and talk for a few more minutes.

I'm leaning against my car door and he's standing in front of me. My feelings are all over the place right now.

"Thank you for the coffee," I say with a smile, "and conversation."

"My pleasure. I hope that we can do it again soon."

Teasingly I say, "I think we can work something out."

"Can we work something out right now?" He's joking but I detect a note of seriousness.

"You're very persistent!"

"How else is a brother supposed to approach a woman like you?"

"Ha-ha, very funny."

"Seriously Natalie, can I see you this weekend? Maybe catch a matinee and have lunch?"

I act as if I'm really thinking about whether or not I'm going to let him take me out.

"I tell you what, if you go to church with me on Sunday, then I'll spend Sunday afternoon with you."

"Cool." He's smiling as if he's won the lottery. I guess I'm doing the same.

"Thanks again for the coffee Miles."

"No, thank you." He pauses. "Natalie?"

"Yes Miles." He's just looking at me, not saying one word. Then he leans down toward me and grabs my face gently between his hands. His hands are soft against my face. He kisses my forehead soft and lingering. Miles smells great, even after a long day. "You have a good evening and drive carefully ok."

"I will Mr. Grey. Good-night."

He opens my car door, makes sure that I'm in safely and waves goodbye. I watch him as he gets into his Jeep. We drive away slowly as if we both want this moment to last.

CHAPTER 3

*O*kay *Natalie, what the hell have you just done? I scream. Ahhh!! Do I have a date on Sunday? Oh God, help me Jesus.*

I try and keep my composure as I'm driving. I slip Babyface into my CD player and listen as he croons out "Whip Appeal." How appropriate. I feel a strange but familiar sensation between my legs. It's not that time of the month. Shit! I just came. What the hell is wrong with me? This is too much for one evening.

Get a grip Nat! He only kissed you on the forehead. You horny, non-sex for two years, hate all men, PMS having, crazy woman.

I need a shower. I speed home. Luckily the traffic is light and there are no cops in sight.

I get to my apartment and am greeted by Pooch my cocker spaniel. "Hey Pooch, how's mama's baby?" I put my briefcase down, kick my shoes off and fall onto my sofa. She runs to the sofa and looks at me with those beautiful eyes. She's waiting for me to give her approval to jump on the sofa with me. "Come on baby!" She jumps on the couch and I grab her and rub her floppy ears.

"Pooch, mommy just came from a date. Well, not an actual date, but an outing. We have a date on Sunday. His name is Miles Grey. He works at the station and he seems really nice. And guess what? He made me come just by kissing my forehead. Can you believe that?" I say while laughing at myself. "Your mommy is outta control." She cocks her head to the side as if to say, "Woman, have you lost it?"

Stop it, stop looking at mommy like I'm crazy. Wait till you see him, you'll see.

I grab her and give her a big hug. "What would I ever do without you?"

I put her down and she walks over to her favorite spot by the fireplace and plops down. I start undressing as I walk into my bedroom. As I'm hanging my suit up, I decide to pick out my clothes for tomorrow. After twenty minutes, I decide on a nice, tan gabardine chemise with a matching jacket that I just bought. It usually takes me less than 10 minutes to select my clothes. *Why so long tonight? Oh, you know why Nat, Miles.*

I light a vanilla candle, run my bath water and put on Sade. As I'm about to step into the tub, my phone rings. I decide to let my answering machine pick up.

"Hey girl, where the hell are you? I've called you twice already. I need to talk to you, it's important. Ciao!"

It's Lela, one of my sisterfriends. I'll call her tomorrow, because she's long-winded and I know I'll need more than thirty minutes. Every time she can't get me immediately, she says it's important. She's a trip, but I love her.

I slide into my Roman tub and let the hot water and smell of vanilla take me away. I go over tonight's events in my mind. I have this nervous, yet delightful feeling in my stomach—and for the life of me, I can't stop smiling. This is so strange for me. I've never been this excited over a man before, at least not on the first meeting. This is too much.

I must have drifted off for a while because my water is cold and I'm looking like a California raisin. I finish bathing and rub vanilla scented oil on my body before I dry off. I love how my skin feels when I do this. I slip on my satin gown and walk into my bedroom. Pooch has made her way into the bedroom and is resting peacefully in her little bed next to mine. I say my prayers and read a chapter of John Grisham's "A Time To Kill." By the time I turn my light off it's 2am, I'm exhausted.

CHAPTER 4

My alarm goes off at 5:30. I hit the snooze button three times before getting up. I roll out of bed and say my prayers. Gotta start each day off right. I put on my exercise gear, wash my face, brush my teeth, grab a Yoplait and head to the gym to meet Taylor.

Taylor and I meet at the gym every morning Monday through Friday no matter what. It's hard as hell waking up this early in the morning, but if I want to keep this hourglass figure, I have to stay at the gym. Traffic is light this time of morning, so it takes me less than 10 minutes to get to the gym. Taylor is pulling into the parking lot at the same time.

"Hey girl!" Her usual perky morning greeting.

"Hey, what's up chick?"

"Ah, nothing and yourself?"

I smile, "A little bit of everything."

"Who is he?" Taylor asks while putting her hands on her hips.

"Who is who?"

Taylor waves a finger in front of my face, "Don't try and play that game with me, I know you. Now who is he? Cuz whoever he is has you cheesing like you won the lotto."

I casually try and play it off. "Oh girl, it's nothing. Just a guy that I work with at the station. We had coffee last night at Starbuck's."

"Coffee, hmmm. Coffee and what else?"

"Just coffee, you crazy woman." We both laugh.

Nudging my arm lightly, "So, do I have to pull your teeth out to get the whole scoop or what? What's he like? How does he look? Has he ever been married? Does he have any kids?"

"Hold up Taylor. You're going to fast and I know that I can't keep anything from Miss Nosey Rosey." Taylor is the nosiest person on the planet, but she has been my friend forever and she has never repeated any of my business. She's been with me through thick and thin. I guess being nosey is her nature and she doesn't mean any harm by it.

"That's right, I gotta know everything! Now give it up."

"Well, he's from Los Angeles, graduated from UNLV, got drafted by the Raiders but hurt his knee. He works as a cameraman at the station. He's tall, handsome, has a great sense of humor and seems to be a really nice guy. And guess what? He's going to church with me on Sunday."

Taylor smiles devilishly. "Ah sookie sookie. Well that's a good sign that he's going to church with you and I hope that he turns out to be nice. I can't believe that you even had coffee with him considering how you feel about men."

"Well, he begged me." I blush.

"He begged you? What does that mean?"

"I mean he got down on his knees and begged me to have a cup of coffee with him."

"Get the fuck outta here!" She's laughing while shaking her head in disbelief.

"No, get the fuck in here. Wasn't that sweet?"

"I swear, men are always falling on their knees for you."

"Yeah, but they don't know what to do once they get down there."

"Girl, I know that's right." We give each other high fives.

"You are so crazy Taylor, that's why I love you. Now let's get in here and burn some fat before we talk the entire morning away."

"You're right, let's go. But I want more details later."

"You got it."

We dash into the gym and work our butts off for two hours before calling it quits. We talk for a few more minutes before getting into our cars. I promise Taylor that I'll call her Sunday evening with all of the details of my date.

When I arrive home, Pooch greets me at the door. She's always happy to see me, no matter how many times in one day. That's the beauty of having a pet. "Hey Pooch, how's my baby?" I pick her up and take her into the kitchen. She licks my cheek. "You're such a sweetie. Do you want some breakfast?" I sit her down and open a can of dog food for her and give her some fresh water. She's in heaven. I begin taking my gym shoes off and the phone rings.

"Good morning."

"Hi beautiful." It's Miles I recognize his voice immediately.

"Hello Miles, how are you this morning?"

"Better now."

Laughing softly, "Well, I'm glad that you're doing so well."

"I hope that you don't mind me calling. We missed exchanging numbers last night, so I got your number from our receptionist at the station. I told her that I had something really important to get to you."

"No, I don't mind. I like a man that knows how to use his resources."

"Do you now?"

"Yes I do. But since you told the receptionist that you had something for me, I'll be expecting something when I see you tonight."

"Man, you are something else lady."

"I try to be." We both laugh.

"Well Natalie, I gotta run. I just wanted to hear your voice and wish you a good day."

"Thanks Miles, that was really sweet of you."

"I'll talk to you later."

"That'll be nice Mr. Grey. Bye-bye."

We hang up and I feel myself getting warm. I run and jump in the shower. *I can't keep getting this way over this man. Oh, stop it Natalie. Enjoy these feelings that you're having, it's ok for a man to make you smile. Yeah, but they always make you cry. Maybe Miles will be different. Maybe.*

I finish showering and turn the radio on to 88.1. They're playing oldies today. The O'Jays are singing *Sadie*. I love that song. The message light is blinking on my answering machine. I press the playback button.

"Hey, it's Naomi. Give me a call when you get in."

"Hi Sister Dear. Hope everything is well. Call me."

"Hey chick, it's Renee. Buzz me later."

"Where the hell are you? I've called you several times. You ain't working that hard. Call me. Love ya." Lela, that girl is so full of drama. I'll call everyone back today.

I look at myself in the mirror and everything is in place. I just need some lipstick and I'll be ready to face the world. Perfect. I grab my briefcase and walk towards the front door. I hear Pooch running through her pet door. I rub her head and say good-bye. I'm off to the mad house.

CHAPTER 5

When I arrive at Saks, everyone is doing their usual thing. Sally and Jesse are gossiping about what fine man Jesse has screwed this week. Jesse Fernandez is this Hispanic, ultra-fickle, ultra-feminine, screw anything with a dick, gay guy who drives me up the wall. Jesse is tall and slender. He's built like a fashion model. He has jet black hair which he wears pulled back into a ponytail. Dresses to the "T" everyday of the week. He is very nice on the eyes, but he works my last nerve. Not because he's gay, but that he's so blatant and detailed about his sexual excursions. Which I might add, are different every two weeks. He shows no shame here at work. True, my girlfriends and I are detailed with each other, but you'd never catch either of us telling our co-workers about how good the sex was last night. That's a big no-no in my book. Anyway, Jesse is jabbering away.

"Girl, he was so fine, I coulda jus ate him up," Jesse says with his very strong accent as he's licking his lips as if he just finished eating something absolutely fabulous.

"Where did you meet this guy Jesse?"

"At a club last night honey."

Sally is stunned. "A one night stand Jesse?" Shaking her head, "Why do you do this to yourself?"

"Nooooo honey chile, this is love. I'll be seeing this sugar daddy tonight." He snaps his fingers.

"Did you wear a condom?"

"For the first hour. Then shit, it got too good!" Jesse grabs his stomach as he laughs.

"Jesse you need to be careful, it's far too dangerous out there for you to be careless." Sally really loves Jesse. They are really close and she has spoke with him often about his careless lifestyle, but he never listens.

Jesse leans and kisses Sally on the cheek. "I know babydoll, but hey if the plague gets me it's just my time, cuz I gotta live!" Jesse starts dancing around like he's at a club, seeming completely oblivious to the advice. Sally just shakes her head again. I greet the two of them.

"Good morning everyone."

"Hey Miss Thang," Jesse says with a wink, "with yo' fine self."

"I can't believe you noticed." Smiling mischievously.

"Oooh, no you didn't go there."

"Oh, yes I did."

"Girl, you are too much." He laughs.

"Somebody has to be. Now do something productive, like a new display of the Fall line of sweaters."

"The boss has spoken. I'll jump on that immedia-mente!" he says in the most dramatic way.

"Thank you Jesse. And how are you Sally?"

"I'm fine Natalie, just a little worn after talking with Jesse. How about you?"

"I'm wonderful Sally." I walk towards my office.

"Hey Natalie, do you still want me to give breaks in lingerie today?"

I turn back, "Yes, and by the way Sally, thanks for being so flexible."

"No problem. Anything for you." She smiles and starts assisting Jesse with his display.

I really like Sally. She's my one employee who never complains and is always dependable. Sally is the epitome of a prep. She has fire red hair that she keeps bobbed just above her ears, freckles, very little make-up and only wears Liz Claiborne and Ralph Lauren clothes. She has more navy in her wardrobe than the United States Air Force, but that's my girl. I wish all of my employees were like Sally. I take a deep breath a begin tackling the paperwork on my desk. Before my day is over I will have fired two employees, interviewed four people and evaluated three. Not to mention settled disputes amongst the employees. Who's not doing what, blah blah. I'm exhausted just thinking about it.

The phone rings. "Hello, this is Natalie."

"Natalie, I have an irate customer on the phone. She wants to return an After Five dress. I've explained to her a thousand times that our formal dresses cannot be returned and she just won't listen. She wants to speak to the boss."

"Thanks, Kim. I'll handle it." I spend half an hour on the phone with this woman and finally decide to give her forty percent of the cost of the dress in store credit. She's not very happy with that, but I explain to her that it's forty percent or nothing. She takes the store credit. Another satisfied customer. I smile as I hang up the phone.

It's 5:30pm and time for me to head to the station. My day just flew by. I take my last stroll through the store to make sure everything is in order. I say goodnight to my co-workers, freshen up and prepare myself for the rush hour crowd. People are really a trip during this time of day. Everybody is so anxious. They drive like animals. Not only do you have to watch where you are going, but you have to watch the car next to you. It's a trip, but I manage to get through it Monday through Friday. I put Sade in my CD player, God I love her! "Jezebel, wasn't born with a silver spoon in her mouth," I sing, "she probably had less than anyone——What the hell!" A car swerves in front of me, nearly knocking me off the freeway. "Oh Lord, please get me to work in one piece!" I say out loud.

I manage to get to the station in less than thirty minutes, which is short of a miracle. I pull into the parking lot and notice how empty this parking lot is during the evening. As I'm getting out of my car I feel as if someone is watching me. I turn around and there he is, sitting in the back of the station van just looking at me. I feel my stomach get a little tingly.

Keep your composure Nat. Keep it cool. You're not affected by this cafe latte hunk.

I walk toward him, not too fast and not too slow, just at a pace to let him get a good look at me, and boy is he looking.

"Hello." I say.

"Hi there." The words just roll off his tongue so smoothly. He smiles.

"So, how are you Miles?"

"I'm good, now that I'm seeing you." He's smiling at me again.

"Well, I'm glad I could brighten your day." I'm nervous.

"You look very nice today, then again, you always look nice."

"Thank you." I smile, he grabs my hands and says, "I love your smile."

"Oh, do you?" I reply.

"Yes, very much so," he says, "and by the way, I have something for you."

He lets go of my hand, reaches into his duffle bag and pulls out a gift-wrapped box.

"What is this?"

"Well, you said that I needed to have something for you when you came to work…so, here is your something."

I unwrap the box and open it. It's a collection of Robert Browning Poems. A bookmark is marking one of the pages in the book. I'm smiling and before I can say anything he takes the book out of my hands and opens the book to where the bookmark is placed, and begins reading.

"*Life In A Love.*" He pauses for moment.

"Escape me? Never, beloved. While I am I, and you are you, so long as the world contains us both, me the loving and you the loth. While the one eludes, must the other pursue. My life is a fault at last, I fear. It seems too much like a fate, indeed. Though I do my best I shall scarce succeed. But what if I fail of my purpose here? It is but to keep the nerves at strain. To dry one's eyes and laugh at a fall, and baffled, get up and begin again. So the chase takes up one's life, that's all. While, look but once from your farthest bound at me so deep in the dust and dark. No sooner the old hope drops to ground than a new one, straight to the self-same mark. I shape me, ever, removed!"

His voice is so calming and poetic. It's gentle, yet I sense his strength. His strength is not overbearing. Not rough as if he has to prove that he's a man. It's subtle, yet it makes you feel safe to be around him. I can't believe he just read poetry to me. I'm melting. I'm slightly taken aback, but trying to appear calm.

"For you." He hands me the book.

"Thank you Miles, this is so sweet of you."

"And the poem?"

"Oh, I loved it. How did you know that I liked Robert Browning?"

"I didn't, but I've always admired his work and I wanted to share something, rather a part of who I am with you."

"Well, I'm shocked, but pleasantly."

'I'm glad." He takes my hand again and kisses my palm and just holds my hand against his lips.

"So, this is a part of you, huh?"

"Just a small part."

"Interesting."

"I can be." We both smile. He lets go of my hand and says, "Have a good evening, I gotta get going, I have a shoot at the Mirage. So, I'll catch you after the news."

"Okay." He closes the van doors and walks toward the front of the van to get in.

"Miles?"

"Yeah?" He says while turning to face me.

"Thanks again for the gift, it was very nice of you."

"The pleasure was all mine." We're both flushed now. As I walk away, I look over my shoulder. He's watching me. I wave goodbye and walk into the newsroom.

CHAPTER 6

I'm sitting at my desk contemplating about what just happened outside. *What is he trying to do to me? What does he want? He can't really be into Robert Browning.* I grab the book and read the poem again. "*Life In A Love.*" How beautiful. I turn to the front of the book and he's written something on the inside cover.

Natalie, I long for a life in a love…a splendid, romantic, unconditional type of love. I won't rush or force it nor will I back down from it if it blows my way. Be my wind! Miles G.

"Ahhhh!" I scream out loud. I can't contain my emotions, this is too much. Everyone in the newsroom turns and looks at me as if I've lost my mind. "Oh, I'm sorry!" I say while grinning from ear to ear.

"Let me read it, whatever it is!"

"Rhonda, just ignore me. I'm losing it."

"Yeah, I can see that, but whatever you're losing it's doing you some good because you are glowing."

I chuckle. "Anyway, how are you Rhonda?"

"Couldn't be better. Life is grand with the exception of the political bullshit around here." Rhonda flips her blond hair back. "Did you hear what happened today?" Rhonda asks as she pulls a chair up to my desk.

"No, I'm just getting to work."

Whispering. "Susan got bumped from 5:30 evening anchor to 5 am anchor. Low blow, huh?"

"Wow, I can't believe that. I'm sure she's not a happy camper about now."

"Hell no, she is pissed! She was crying earlier. There is no way that I would have let those pricks see me cry. I'm sure she'll be outta here soon. Hint, hint." She winks at me.

"Hint, hint what Rhonda?"

"Hint, hint two slots will be open and you can fill one of those slots." She's smiling her little devilish smile.

"Yeah right. I barely get to do any packages as it is around here."

"Listen here sweetie, everyone has to pay their dues. You'll get your chance real soon. Frank likes you, I can tell. And when you get right down to it, that's all that matters." She pats my shoulder and says, "You'll be anchoring soon! Mock my words."

"Knock on wood." I say as I knock on my desk.

"Later chick, I gotta go put on my face. See ya in the studio." Rhonda gets up and strolls to her personal dressing room.

"Later Barbie." She turns back and smiles.

Rhonda Baxter has been the top anchor at KVBC for eight years now. She's a walking Barbie doll. Blond hair, blue eyes, size four and everyone here hates her. They say she's the bitch of the year, but obviously management loves her. From the first day I arrived, Rhonda and I hit it off. She's always been very nice to me. She's pretty fickle and shallow most of the time. It's all about money when it comes to Rhonda. Period. She doesn't beat around the bush when it comes to the American dollar. She's been going to re-hab about a year now for cocaine. Her family is filthy rich. Word is that her father bought her this job. Whatever the case, she's a damn good anchorwoman.

I walk over to the assignment desk and get today's scoop from Jay Waters our assignment editor, and find out what my beat is this evening. When you're part-time you cover whatever needs to be covered. While Jay and I are talking, something important comes over the scanner. There's been a shooting on Donna Street. Donna Street is one of the worst gang area in North Las Vegas. Crip territory. Jay looks around and sees no one but me. Evenings are usually like this.

Jay listens closely to the scanner, turns to me and says, "Natalie, go cover this. If it's really big, we might go live." I can't believe my ears. "Live! Jay I've never done a live shoot before!"

"Well Nat, there's a first time for everything, and you're the only person I can send. You know how Frank feels about one anchor doing the news and Amy went home sick. You're it!" My heart is beating like crazy.

I can't believe that Jay is sending me to cover such a big story. Shit! Okay Nat, get it together. You can't mess up this opportunity.

Miles is back from his shoot at the hotel. As he's walking through the door, Jay shouts at Miles, "Hey Miles, there's been a shooting over on Donna Street."

"Yeah, I heard it over the scanner."

"Well, I'm sending Natalie to cover this one and if it's big, let's do a live okay?'

"Cool, we're outta here." Looking in my direction, "Natalie you ready?"

Still in shock and nervous as hell, I manage to get out, "Yeah." I grab my pen and pad and follow Miles out the door. He opens the van door for me to get in and then walks around to the driver's side. "So, I finally get a chance to work with you." I don't respond. "Hey Nat, what's wrong?"

"What's wrong? Everything!" I throw my hands up. "I've never done a live shoot before. I'm nervous as hell. What if I screw up? Miles I can't mess this up! I have to do a good job!" Miles grabs my hand and calmly says, "Listen up, I've done live shoots a thousand times, there's nothing to it. It's not hard. All you have to do is follow my lead and I'll walk you through everything. Natalie, you are a good reporter. Think of this as an extended package. You're just in front of the camera longer. You'll do fine

"Ok, if you say so." For the first time in my life I'm having doubts about myself. *Why now? I've hungered for this moment. Why am I so nervous?*

"I do, now let's get this over with." Miles winks at me, starts the van and we head towards Donna Street.

CHAPTER 7

We arrive at Donna Street in rapid time. Thank god the station isn't that far from North Las Vegas. I grew up in North Las Vegas. It used to be the place to live for black families trying to move away from the drugs and violence in West Las Vegas. It was one of the first really diverse areas in Las Vegas. I had a wonderful childhood and some of my best memories were playing on Donna Street with my cousins when the projects weren't a bad place to live. How the years have changed things. Gangs have popped up everywhere in Vegas and Donna Street is where the major action is on a nightly basis.

Dozens of squad cars are surrounding the Donna Street Apartments. Miles parks the van and gets his equipment while I take a few breaths before stepping out of the van. I scan the crowd to see if I see any familiar faces. I do. I spot Officer Carrington, a neighborhood cop I've known for years. He'll give me the entire scoop. I motion Miles to follow me.

"Hey Officer C."

"Hey baby, how's my other daughter?" Officer C gives me a big hug and kisses me on the cheek.

"I'm doing good. How are you? I haven't seen you in few weeks?"

Smiling. "You know me, I'm hangin' in there. I'll have to tell the Mrs. that I saw you, she just mentioned yesterday that she needed to make your favorite cookies."

"Give her my love and tell her that I'll be by soon for cookies." We both laugh.

"Oh," while grabbing Miles' arm, "Mr. C this is Miles, Miles Mr. C." They greet and shake hands.

"Can you tell me what happened Mr. C?"

"Well, about an hour ago we got a call about some shots being fired. When we got here, four people had been shot. They're all alive except two are in critical condition. The young man allegedly responsible for the shootings is holding one of the victims family hostage inside that apartment." Officer C points in the direction of a group of officers standing behind a roped off area.

"Does anyone know the motive?"

"It appears to be gang related. Last week two Bloods were shot near Gerson Park and they were homeboys of the guy whose holding this family hostage." Officer C shakes his head in disgust. "We're just killing ourselves, it's a damn shame."

"I know, it's really sad. These young brothers are practicing genocide and don't even know it or better yet they don't even care." I pause to make a few notes. "Do we know how many are inside?"

"We're not sure, but we think it's between three and seven people. We've talked to a few neighbors and they've given us a list of people they believe may be inside, but no one is quite sure."

I continue to take notes and ask questions while Miles is shooting footage. "Has the young man talked to you or any of the other officers?"

"Yeah, he yelled out the door earlier to find Charley Boy and he'll talk."

"I take it Charley Boy is the one who shot his home-boys.

"That's the word."

"Thanks Officer C, I'll talk to you later. Let me see what else I can find out." I hug Officer C and take off towards the crowd.

"Be careful!" Officer Carrington yells.

"I will."

I notice hundreds of people standing around, mostly African Americans. However, there are a few Hispanics in the crowd. As I walk through the crowd, I try and find the most intelligent and appropriate looking person to ask a few questions. Not the woman with pink rollers in her head and rabbit house shoes on or the brother with no front teeth who's drinking a 40-ounce who swears he saw the whole thing. I hate when I'm watching the news and the reporter has selected the worst black in the crowd to interview. It's as if there is a shortage of intelligent black folk to interview when white reporters arrive in the hood, but I don't have problem finding black folk in the hood who can speak without saying "dese" "dat" and "doze." That's why my policy will always be to show my people in the most positive light regardless of the situation.

Her name is Deborah Coleman. She's a middle-aged black woman, hair slightly gray, not overweight but thick, dressed in a nice floral sundress and flat sandals. She's holding a little girl in her arms. "I was sitting across the street in the park with my granddaughter when this green Monte Carlo pulls up. A young man around sixteen or seventeen years old gets out of the car. There were four young men standing over there." She points in the direction of the roped off apartment. "They were just talking and laughing when this guy gets out of the car and starts shooting." She is very upset and there are tears in her eyes. "I was so scared! I just grabbed my granddaughter and hit the ground. What's wrong with these people? Why are they killing each other?" She wipes her tears and switches her grandchild on her other hip. "My god, my grandbaby can't even play outside without gunshots going off. It's so sad." I wrap my arms around her while she cries. I can only imagine her fear, yet I know how she feels when it comes to our people killing each other. It's a pain that most blacks have learned to live with because we hear about it every day.

Miles continues to shoot footage while I thank Ms. Coleman for her interview. People start running towards me and jumping in front of the camera, "Hey sistah, I saw everything, come talk to me!" "He don't know nuthin, I know everything!" "That mutha fuckas crazy, let me tell you what happened." Miles shuts down the camera and I listen to a few others put in their two cents before heading towards the crime scene. *I don't know why people lose their minds when they see television cameras.*

CHAPTER 8

As I'm walking up the sidewalk, I feel as if I'm walking in water, but it hasn't rained. I look down at my feet and I'm standing in a pool of blood. I feel faint.

"Oh, Miles look!"

"Natalie, stay calm. I'm right here. It's going to be alright. Walk on the grass." I take his directive and step onto the grass. My heart is beating a mile a minute.

"I feel sick."

"You'll be ok, just don't look down," Miles says.

"Yeah, right."

Two of the young men that have been shot are being carted away in ambulances, the other two are being patched up and questioned by police. Their shirts are covered with blood. I realize at this moment that I do not want to be a crime reporter. Period.

There are several reporters roving around trying to get the scoop. I notice Nathan McCall from Channel 13 interviewing the woman with pink rollers and Pamela

Keeve from Channel 8 is talking to a similar breed. *Maybe it's a white thang. I swear I hate that shit.*

I take a closer look at the two young men being questioned. Neither of them look a day over 16. My heart is bleeding. *What is happening to our men?*

"Natalie, you alright?' Miles asks while sitting his gear down.

"Yeah, I'm ok. I just got caught up in the moment."

"It can happen sometimes, but don't let it get to you." Miles looks at me and I can tell that he has numbed himself to situations like this. He's probably had to shoot dozens of crime scenes. Sooner or later a guess one can't help but to become numb.

Miles gets a call that Jay wants to go live.

"We're gonna go live. Where do you want to do it?"

"Right here is fine, but let's try and get closer to the apartment." Miles sets up his equipment and instructs me on everything that he wants me to do. He doesn't treat me like a novice, but comes across very patient and considerate of my nervousness. All communication between myself and the anchors is complete. Rhonda will introduce me. I take my peach compact out of my pocket, powder my nose and make sure that my hair is in place. *Thank god for 12- hour lipstick.*

"Ready cutie?" he asks. I blush slightly at Miles' flirting.

"As ready as I'm going to be." *This is do or die Nat. Break a leg.*

Back at the station, Rhonda and Don are beginning the 11 o'clock news.

'Good evening, I'm Rhonda Baxter."

"And I'm Don Stewart."

"We have breaking news this evening. There has been a shooting on Donna Street in North Las Vegas. Reporter Natalie Norwood is at the scene. Natalie can you tell us what happened?"

"Well Rhonda, according to police and witnesses, a green Monte Carlo pulled in front of the Donna Street Apartments. A young man got out of the vehicle and started shooting at four young men that were standing outside the complex talking. Afterwards, the gunman ran into this apartment directly behind me and is presently holding several people hostage."

Donald: Natalie, do police think that this is gang related?

Natalie: Yes. Police believe that this shooting is in retaliation to the shooting last week in Gerson Park involving Crips and Bloods.

Rhonda: What is the status of the victims?

Natalie: Two of the victims have minor injuries and two are in critical condition.

Don: Natalie, what do we know about the gunman and the hostages?

Natalie: We know that the gunman is allegedly a member of the Gerson Park Bloods and that he is holding hostage family members of the gang rival that he believes shot his homeboy.

Rhonda: Has the gunman spoken to police yet?

Natalie: Yes. In fact he told officers to find a young man by the name of Charley Boy and he would talk. Charley Boy is who he believes did the shooting last week.

Don: Have the officers located this Charley Boy?

Natalie: Not as of yet. But just one second.

I turn towards the noise behind. Someone has opened the apartment door and is motioning for an officer to come closer. More police squad cars have arrived. Guns are raised everywhere. This is indeed a war zone. Miles shoots everything while a give Rhonda and Don a detailed account of what is taking place.

"Apparently, he is yelling at the officer to take his gun off before approaching the apartment. The officer that's walking towards the door is Officer Steve Carrington, one of the most visible officers in this community. Officer Carrington is removing his gun. He is placing his gun on the ground. He is slowly walking towards the apartment. He is talking to someone at the door. We can't get a clear picture of whose at the door. Officer Carrington is walking back. He's walking towards us."

Officer Carrington stops in front of me and takes my hand. "He wants you to come inside. He wants to get a message to Charley Boy by television and he wants you." Officer C looks worried.

"He wants me to come inside?" My voice quivers.

"Listen Natalie, this young man is dangerous. You do not have to do this. We do not want to put you or your cameraman in danger. We can handle this." The camera is still rolling when the gunman comes to the door and yells, "Send her in now or I'll kill every person in this joint!"

"Natalie, we can try and negotiate with this guy or find some other way to handle this situation. Please do not go in there. I'm begging you."

"Officer C, as nervous and scared as I am, I cannot risk innocent lives. If I can get them out safe, then I have to go in. I have to try. Those people inside do not deserve to die." I turn back towards the camera. "Rhonda and Don, we're going inside. We'll keep the camera rolling.

I look at Miles, he sees the fear in my eyes but his eyes tell me that he's with me all of the way. "Do you really want to do this?" Miles asks.

"No, but I have to."

"Well, let's go." Miles follows me with the camera as dozens of police officers surround us and Officer C goes over some precautionary measures.

Rhonda: Oh my god, ladies and gentlemen as you can see our reporter Natalie Norwood has been demanded by the gunman to come inside of the apartment where he is allegedly holding hostages. Our prayers are with Natalie and our cameraman Miles Gray. We are going postpone all programming and stay live on the scene."

Don: This is unbelievable. Shootings. Hostages. And now two of our own.

Rhonda: She's heading into the apartment. Natalie, can you hear us?

Natalie: Yes I can Rhonda.

Don: Natalie, please be careful.

Natalie: I will.

I quickly say a prayer and walk with Miles up to the apartment.

The door opens slowly. I can't see his face. We step inside. The door closes behind us. My heart drops.

CHAPTER 9

The apartment is dimly lit, with the exception of the kitchen light. The smell of urine reeks through the room. There is a brown tattered sofa in the living room that's spotted and torn; probably from the years of use and neglect. Trash is on the floor and food is everywhere. Spilled ketchup, dried up eggs in a skillet, chicken bones, dirty diapers, empty and half-filled bottles of beer and soda. Roaches are having a family reunion on the walls and I am trying not to throw up.

Five people are sitting on the floor; three children and two women. The children look as if they haven't had a bath or their hair combed in days. The women are older, probably in their early or mid-fifties. Both women look as if they might have been very attractive in their younger days, but obviously have lived rough, hard lives. They are crying and fear is in their eyes. The children are really too young to fully understand what is taking place around them, but are frightened because there is a stranger that is making them sit on the floor and not say a word, and the two people that they do know are crying. Poor babies.

It dawns on me that ever since I walked through the door it's been completely silent, and I've been so busy taking in my surroundings that I forgot that there's another person in the room. I quickly turn around and there he is just leaning against the door, holding his gun, and staring at me with those eyes. Eyes that say nothing yet say so much. Eyes that are cold and heartless yet know pain. Eyes of child, but also of a man. He's the color midnight. Almost blue-black. His skin is flawless. His hair is closely cropped and wavy. He's beautiful.

He's dressed in baggy black jeans with an oversized red sweatshirt and red Nikes. If I had to guess, I'd say he was no older than fifteen. He has this baby face that's not fully developed yet, but there is a sense of hardness and tension that shadows his face. *What happened to this baby? What has brought him to this point? I wonder?*

"Listen, I ain't gonna hurt y'all aiight. I just gotta get my message out, and you guys were here. So why not milk yawl!" I look at him in shock, anger, and disgust. I'm feeling so many things right now. He's waving his gun as he's talking. "So, how long is it gonna take for you guys to set up?"

"We're ready when you are." Miles replies.

"Hey Nat, why don't you guys sit on the couch." I give Miles the kind of look that says, "If you think that I am sitting on that roach infested clubhouse, forget it!"

But he gives me the kind of look that says, "Sit your prissy ass down and do your fucking job. You can always get another suit." I sit down. The gunman walks towards the couch and sits next to me.

"What's your name?" I ask while flipping through my writing pad.

"Killer."

"Killer?"

"Yeah Killer." He's laughing. "I know what you're thinking."

"And what is that?"

"You want to know why my name is Killer, huh?"

"Would you like to tell me why your name is Killer?" I say slightly sarcastic.

"Yeah, they call me Killer cuz I'll kill any muthafucka that crosses me." His tone suggests that he's quite proud of his reputation and pretty souped on himself.

"Mmmm, well Killer, is that how you'd like me to introduce you?"

"Yeah! Fuck yeah!" He's really excited about this.

"What's your real name Killer?"

"Why? Who wants to know?" He snaps angrily.

"I'd like to know. I need to know your name in order to do this story"

"Aiight, my name is Antonio Jones."

"Well Antonio, don't you think that your real name may be more appropriate when I introduce you?"

"Yeah, maybe you right. But listen, when I say what I gotta say, I'm gonna say Killer ok?"

"That's fine."

I'm paying close attention to his mannerism, his speech, his tone, everything. He's a baby trying to be a man and doesn't even have a clue about manhood. *Or does he? Maybe I'm assuming too much?* This is so sad. The hostages are still sitting on the floor. The babies are becoming restless and want to get up, but the women are holding them close to them. I look over at the women and try to reassure them with my eyes. They are still terrified.

"Antonio, what exactly do you want from us?"

He thinks to himself for a moment and says, "I want to get the word out to that muthafucka that I'm gonna kill his whole goddamn family if he doesn't come and face me like a man."

"Do you think that this is being a man?" I'm very careful with my tone at this point because I don't know if he'll snap.

"Whatcha mean?"

"Do you think holding innocent women and children hostage is being a man?"

"Gotta do whatcha gotta do."

"It doesn't make it right."

"Fuck being right,'" he stands and starts pacing the floor, "that punk didn't think about right when he gunned down my homies. So fuck being right, it's about gettin even." He holds the gun up to me and says, "Enough talk, let's get this thing rollin'." I jump slightly. I've never been this close to a gun. He laughs at the fact that I'm a little shaken. "I ain't gone hurt you babygirl." He sits back down on the couch and stares at Miles. "Hey man, who duh fuck you talkin' to?"

"Just the guys at the television station man. I'm setting everything up."

"Aiight, aiight. Cool. I jus don't want no shit. You got it?" He points the gun towards Miles.

"Yeah. I got it." Miles says while continuing to do his job without skipping a beat.

I take a deep breath and look up at Miles. He mouths to me to stay calm. I slowly regain my composure. *You're going to be ok Natalie. Stay professional.*

Miles has everything set up. He has been very calm throughout this ordeal, it's almost as if he's been in this type of situation before. Miles cues me and I hear Rhonda and Don. "Good-evening ladies and gentlemen, earlier tonight we informed you about four young men being gunned down on Donna Street in North Las Vegas. According to authorities, two of the men have minor injuries the other two are in critical condition. The gunman is holding an entire family along with our reporter Natalie Norwood and cameraman Miles Johnson hostage. We're going to go live on location inside of the apartment."

"Natalie, can you hear us?"

"Yes Don, I can."

"How are you and the others doing?"

"We're doing okay, everyone is doing fine."

"We understand that the young man would like to talk."

"Yes Don. I'm here with Antonio Jones. Antonio, what would you like to say?"

I hold the microphone towards him. He looks directly into the camera and says, "Yeah, cool. Uh, my name is Antonio Jones, better known as Killer. First of all I'd like to throw a shout out to my homies in Gerson, hey motha-fuckas what's up?" He throws up his gang sign.

"Antonio, remember that we are on television." I say calmly.

"Aiight, my bad. Anyway, what I got to say is this: This message is for Charley Boy. Yeah niggah, if you're listening to this message listen good and hard. If you don't get your ass, I mean get your butt home within the next hour, I'm gonna blow your whole family away. You got that? Your whole family." Miles zooms in on the family still sitting on the floor.

"Is there anything else Antonio?"

"Naw, that's it for now."

"Well Rhonda and Don, you've heard it first. Antonio is threatening to kill this entire family if this Charley Boy doesn't arrive within the hour."

Donald: Natalie, who is Charley Boy?

Natalie: Don, Charley Boy is the person who allegedly shot and killed Antonio's homeboys last week in Gerson Park."

Antonio snatches the microphone from me, "Hey, he ain't alledgedly shit. He shot my boys. What is all this alleged shit?"

"Okay Antonio, it's just that there hasn't been a trial yet and as reporters we have to say alleged."

"Well, it ain't no alleged. I saw the niggah do wit my own eyes. Turn that shit off."

"Okay, okay." I say softly while removing the mic from his hands. I motion Miles to turn the camera off. Unbeknownst to me he doesn't turn the camera off, but fakes it. Everyone watching this newscast will see everything that follows.

CHAPTER 10

"You guys can make yourself at home, cuz you gonna be here for a while." Antonio cheerfully says while flopping on the couch as if this is a big joke.

"Oh, we sincerely appreciate your generosity." I say. My patience with this kid is growing thin, and I feel myself tensing up. This nervousness in my stomach is driving me crazy.

"You know what?" he asks me. "You have a smart fuckin mouth and I hate smart ass bitches!"

"First of all, I can give less that a damn about what you hate. Second, remember your mama the next time you call a sistah a bitch." *Natalie what are you doing? Are you crazy? This boy can blow your head off!*

Antonio's eyes widen with hatred and before I know it he rushes me and knocks me flat on my back. He straddles me and puts the gun to my head.

"Shut the fuck up or I'll blow your fuckin' head off! I mean it!" I see Miles moving towards Antonio. "Mutha fucka make my day!" Antonio says while aiming his gun towards Miles.

"Listen brotha, we don't want any problems. Just calm down. Don't hurt the sistah." Antonio gets off of me and starts pacing the room again. "Well, you need to tell yo sistah to just stick to reporting and keep her mouth shut!"

"I hear ya man." Miles says as he walks over to the family and starts talking to them. "Hey man, what you talkin' bout to them?" Antonio asks as he walks up to Miles.

"Just keeping them calm. That's all. Is it ok if the kids have something to drink and go to the bathroom?"

"Yeah, you go and get them something to drink and smart mouth can take them to the bathroom. Remember any funny stuff and everyone dies."

Miles walks into the cramped kitchen and finds some juice in the refrigerator. He pours it into two cups while I grab the hands of the two little girls and take them into the bathroom. "Leave the bathroom door open." Antonio yells.

I lean down and re-assure the girls that everything will be ok. They each use the restroom and I wash their hands. There are no clean towels in sight, so I dry their hands on my jacket. The older of the two starts to cry. I pick her up.

"Sweetie, don't cry. It's going to be all right. I promise." I kiss her on her cheek and wipe her tears. "Let's get some juice." Her eyes come alive at the mention of juice. I put her down and she grabs my hand tightly. We walk back into the room and Miles hands them their juice. I don't know what takes over me, but I feel as if I'm about to explode. I turn and look at Antonio and quickly walk up to him.

"Man, you better sit yo ass down!" He takes a few steps back. I continue towards him until there's about two feet between us.

"No, you sit down! I am so sick of this. If you are going to shoot me then do it, but don't keep waving that gun in front of my face. No one in this room has done anything to you, and yet you're willing to kill us over some bullshit. And you'll be the first to yell "the white man" when this is all over." I start pacing the floor hysterically. "Well, ain't no white man in here. It's just us. Black folk. And I am sick and tired of young black brothers killing each other over nonsense. Neighborhoods, turf. None of you own one piece of property and got the nerve to be fighting over shit that don't belong to you. Now how stupid is that? It's crazy! Wake up! When are you going to wake up?" I start to cry. I can't help it. My body is shaking because I'm really terrified, and I don't know what Antonio is going to do. Everyone in the room is looking at me in shock, even Antonio who is mad as hell. Miles is shaking his head in disbelief and has this smirk on his face.

"Shut the fuck up, I ain't gonna tell you no mo!" He gets in my face. So close that our noses are nearly touching, but I'm ok. Even though I'm still shaking, I'm ok.

"No Antonio, I'm not going to shut up. I want you to talk to me." I say softly.

Stepping away from me. "What you wanna talk about? I ain't got nuthin' to say to you." I turn and sit on the couch and motion for him to sit next to me. He hesitates, but he sits on the other end of the couch. I try and speak in a very soft, loving tone so that he won't become too defensive.

"Antonio, do you love yourself?"

"What you mean? Yeah I love myself?"

"Who else loves you?"

"This shit is crazy!" he throws his hands up.

"I'm serious, who else loves you?" This question really bothers him for some reason.

"Shit, I don't know."

"You mean to tell me that you can't think of anyone else in this world that loves you?"

He looks slightly baffled as if he's never thought about this before now.

"Naw, just my homies."

"What about your family?"

"I ain't got no family lady. I been on my own since I was 12. My family is my boys."

"Where's your mom and dad?"

Disgusted. "Man, mom's smoked out and I ain't never met my dad." Even though he's trying to be tough, I can see the pain in his eyes. I'm sure that he has a good heart, but has never been taught how to use it. He's leaning with his elbows on his knees. I slide closer to him. He jumps. I touch his arm.

"Listen Antonio, I'm not going to try anything. I just want to talk." He relaxes a little.

"What do you want to be in life Antonio?"

He hunches his shoulders.

"You never thought about it?"

Barely audible, "Sometimes, but not often. I mean why should I? I ain't gonna live a long life."

"Why would you say a thing like that?"

Tears are welling in his eyes. "Cuz, my life is fucked up. Always has been and always will be." *God, this is so sad.*

"Your life doesn't have to be this way Antonio."

"Lady, you crazy!"

"Natalie. My name is Natalie," I interject softly.

"Well Natalie, after this they gonna lock me up for life. I might as well kill myself right now." He holds the gun to his head. I reach for his hand and just hold it in mine. I can feel the gun. I slowly pull his hand down from his head and place it in his lap.

"Antonio, life is what you make it. We all have different circumstances that we are born into. Some good. Some bad. But the road we choose is entirely up to us. You may not have had the best parents on earth and yes you've been on the streets since you were twelve, you have always had to look out for you and that's messed up. But regardless of what has happened to you, you do know right from wrong. This is wrong." I point around the room. "These women and babies have not caused any harm to you. They do not deserve to die." Snatching his hand away.

"My homeboys didn't deserve to die neither."

"This is true, but killing everyone in this room is not going to bring your homeboys back to life."

"But I'll feel a whole lot better knowing that I got someone close to that niggah."

"Antonio." Squeezing his hand. "Please don't do this sweetie. Don't mess up your life."

"I ain't got no life lady. Don't you understand? Damn!" He throws his hands up again and stares at me like a lost pup. A few tears fall from his eyes and he quickly wipes them away. He's embarrassed that he shed a few tears in front of us.

"You do have a life. You just haven't had the chance to live it in a normal, loving way." I grab his hand again. This time he doesn't jump. "Don't throw your life away. You can make some changes. Let me help you," I plead.

"Why you wanna help? You don't know me," he says while hitting his chest.

"No, I don't know you, but I see something special in you. I don't want to see another brother go to jail and waste his life. Let me help you. Whatever I can do to help you get through this, I'm willing to do." I reach for his gun. He hesitates.

"You not just talkin' so you can leave and get me jacked, are you?" His eyes are begging me not to forsake him.

"Antonio, you have my word. I promise that I'll be here for you." I reach for the gun again. This time he hands it to me. I sit the gun on the couch next to me and wrap my arms around him as he starts to cry. *My god he's just a baby.* I gently touch his face and tell him that everything will be ok. I look towards Miles and he's walking the family out of the apartment.

"Natalie?" Antonio grabs my hand. "I'm scared, I'm really scared. I really fucked up."

"Things are going to be fine." The police barge in and ask Antonio to lie on the floor. I tell the police that it's not necessary, that his gun is sitting next to me.

"Maam, it's procedure. We have to handcuff him. Please step away from him." One of the officers grabs my arm and leads me away. "No, please don't, let me walk with him." The officers have handcuffed Antonio and seem to be handling him quite rough. He isn't resisting. He just looks at me. Officer Carrington walks into the apartment.

"Officer C, please don't let them hurt him, he's not a bad kid."

"Natalie, calm down. This is procedure. He committed a serious crime tonight and we have to follow procedure, but he's going to be ok."

"Can I come to the station with him? Please Mr. C. I'm begging you."

"Let me see what I can do." We all walk out of the apartment. People are gathered everywhere. They're pointing, yelling and staring. I watch two of the officers escort Antonio to the squad car. He turns back and looks at me. I run up to him and one of the officers stops me in my tracks.

"I'm coming to the station as soon as I finish up here ok?"

"Yeah, aiight." He lowers his head and steps into the car. I watch them pull off.

CHAPTER 11

I turn around and scan the crowd looking for Miles. He's standing a few feet away talking to the folks back at the station. He calls out my name.

"You ready to wrap up here?"

"Am I ever!"

"Listen Natalie, I'm really proud of you. It took an awful lot of courage to do what you did tonight. You got heart. I like that in you."

"Thanks Miles. I'm just glad that you were with me. I felt protected having you near."

"Well, you handled your business. You did what a good reporter needed to do and I just ran the camera. You really didn't need me." He chuckles.

"Oh yes I did. If things would have gotten out of hand, shoot, I don't even want to think about it. I'm just glad that things turned out ok."

"Me too, good work."

"Thank you."

"Let's wrap this up little lady. Oh, here's some info that I got from one of the officers." Miles hands me a small notepad. I quickly scan his notes, powder my face and take a deep breath. The light goes on.

"Good evening. We're here live at the Donna Street Apartments in North Las Vegas where several persons were held hostage including myself and my cameraman. Four people were shot and their names are being withheld until family members have been notified. The shootings, the hostage situation are all in retaliation for two deaths that happened last week. All gang related. The young man responsible for tonight's shooting has been taken into custody.

Rhonda: Natalie, how are the family members doing that were being held with you?

Natalie: They are fine. A little shaken up, but no one was hurt.

Donald: We understand that the gentleman the gunman was waiting for did arrive on the scene.

Natalie: That is correct. He was arrested for connection with the killings that took place last week.

Rhonda: Do we know the ages of the victims?

Natalie: It is estimated that the victims were all between the ages of 15 and 18 years.

Donald: This whole situation is such a tragedy.

Rhonda: It is. However, we at the station are thankful that you and our cameraman Miles Grey are safe.

Natalie: "We're both thankful as well. This is definitely a sign that our young people, specifically our young men, are in danger and in need of guidance. It's time for our community leaders and families to really come together for the sake of saving our youth. Our children are so precious, but how can they survive if they're killing off one another? Five lives are in serious condition tonight, all because of foolishness, because of turf and colors. It's tragic and it must stop. Let's not lose another youth to violence Las Vegas. Reporting live for Channel 3 News, I'm Natalie Norwood." The tears are rolling down my face. I can't seem to stop them. I'm so frustrated and angry. Miles turns the camera off and walks towards me."

"Hey Natalie, don't cry sweetheart, it'll be okay. We all just have to do our part."

"I know Miles, but it's just so sad. I was so scared inside of that apartment. What if we didn't make it?" I feel myself becoming hysterical.

"Hey, we made it ok. It's over now." He whispers gently. We embrace for a few minutes and then get into our van and head back to the television station. On our drive back to the station, Miles informs me that he never turned the camera off while we were inside of the apartment. I couldn't believe it. The entire community saw what took place in there. Wow! When we arrive at the station, I tell Miles to let everyone know that I've gone to the police station to check on Antonio. Miles makes me promise that I'll call him when I get home. This whole situation is just so overwhelming. *I wonder if I can really help this young man. Can he be saved from his own world? I really don't know. I hope so. I can't imagine what he's been through. God help us all.*

CHAPTER 12

I get home around 2a.m. and immediately jump in the shower. I can't believe what just happened tonight. It feels like a dream, but I know that it's real. Antonio was really sad when I left the police station. I promised him that I'd check on him later today. I lather my body and just let the hot water take me away for a few moments. As I'm rinsing off, I hear the phone ring and Pooch starts barking. I rush rinsing off and grab the phone before my answering machine picks up.

"Hello," I say while running back into the bathroom to get my towel.

"Hi there. You're home?"

"Yeah, I just got in about twenty minutes ago."

"How are you?"

"I'm exhausted, overwhelmed, shocked. You name it, I'm feeling it."

"I know what you mean Nat, I still can't get over what happened tonight."

"Miles this is just so unreal, it's really trippin' me out."

"How's Antonio?"

"Not so good. I really feel sorry for him. He just got caught up in his environment."

"Yeah, I know what you mean. I see it every day. Brothas get caught up and there's no one there to teach them another way. It's amazing how one's surroundings affects their whole character, because I really believe that deep down inside Antonio is a good person." I can hear the concern in Miles' voice.

"Yeah, and that's the sad part. His life is practically over because of nonsense and things he literally had no control over," I say.

"What's going to happen to him?"

"Well, we were able to track down his mom, and hopefully she'll get herself together by the time of the hearing on Thursday. Because of the crime, he's not being released on bail. However, I did tell him that I will be in court for him on Thursday."

"That's very kind of you. I'd like to come with you o.k.?"

"That would be nice, he needs as much support as he can get."

"Did the police say anything about this Charley Boy person?"

"Well, when we got to the station he was there too. Apparently, he saw everything on TV and came to the apartments while we were inside. Police arrested him on the spot. Supposedly, he confessed to last weeks shootings."

"Damn. Why didn't the police let us know that he came to the scene?"

"That I do not know, and frankly I don't think my mind can handle knowing much more."

"Well Nat, you better get some rest, you've had a rough day."

"We both have. Thanks for everything Miles, I couldn't have gotten through this without you."

Chuckling. "Yeah, I think you could have, but I'm glad you didn't have to."

"Thanks for calling Miles."

"Sleep well, and I'll talk to you later on today."

"Goodnight."

I slip on my nightgown and get on my knees to say my prayers. "Father God which art in heaven, I come to you thanking you for all of your many blessings and for giving me life. Lord, today was a really rough day for me, but I realize that you have never placed more on me than I can bear. Thank you for allowing no harm to come to the family that was being held this evening nor to Miles and I. A special prayer for Antonio. Lord please give him another chance at life and help his family Lord. I pray for the recovery of those injured. Most of all Lord, I pray for world peace and love. Lastly, that you continue to lead me and guide me in the path that is pleasing unto you. I love you God. Amen."

I feel Pooch next to me. I pick her up. "Hi baby, Mommy's gonna let you sleep with her tonight. Go get your blanket. She runs and grabs her blanket out of her bed. She's so smart. I lay her blanket at the foot of the bed and she hops on top of it. "Good night baby." I get under my covers and stare at the ceiling while going over everything that happened today. After several minutes I reach over and turn my lamp off and fall into a deep sleep.

CHAPTER 13

The sound of the phone ringing startles me. I look at the clock. Who could be calling me at 7:45 in the morning on a Saturday.

"Good morning," I say groggily

"Natalie?"

"Speaking."

"Hi Natalie. Sorry for waking you, it's Frank Holmes."

"Oh, hi Mr. Holmes. How are you?"

"Frank, please."

Sitting up in my bed. "Okay," pausing momentarily, "Frank."

"I'm great! The reason I'm calling you is to let you know that you did a terriffic job last night. My phone has not stopped ringing. *Dateline* wants to interview you."

I know I'm not hearing what I think I'm hearing.

"Mr. Holmes, I mean Frank…you're kidding."

"No, I'm serious. I'll give you all the details on Monday. I'd like to meet with you as soon as you come in, o.k.?"

"No problem." Stunned.

"Natalie?"

"Yes Mr. Holmes."

"The entire station is very proud of you. It took a lot of guts to do what you did."

"Well, thank you, I appreciate that."

"Have a good weekend Natalie and I'll see you on Monday."

"Thanks for calling Mr. Holmes."

"No, thank you. Goodbye!"

"Goodbye."

I can't believe it. A call from Frank Holmes. Frank is the general manager at Channel 3. People are always mistaking him for the ex -Los Angeles Raider player Frank Hawkins. They definitely resemble each other. Frank is a very nice man, always warm and considerate. We've never had any lengthy conversation, but the few that we've had have been pleasant. Everyone at the station adores Frank. I can't believe he called me. And did he say that *Dateline* wants to interview me? This is too much. "Hey Pooch, did you hear that? *Dateline* wants to interview your mommy!" She jumps off the bed and heads toward the door, I let her out for a few. The phone rings again.

"Hello."

"Hey chickaria, you super reporter woman you!" We both burst into laughter.

"Hey Renee. What's up?"

"You, baby cakes! I'm so proud of you. I was so scared something was going to happen to you. Thank God you guys got out safely. So, how do you feel?" When Renee gets excited she talks a mile a minute. I can barely keep up with her, but she is by far one of my sweetest and dearest friends.

"Girl, I feel fine. Just trying to take everything in."

"Yeah, I can only imagine. We all wanted to jump in our cars and come to the scene, but Lela thought that we should stay home by the TV. We all finally agreed that our presence would not have helped the situation and you know yo girl would have been tryin' to bust in there like the National Guard."

"Girl, you are crazy. I know you got my back."

"Well, be expecting a sleu of calls today, cuz everyone wants to talk to you, o.k.?

"Alright chick, thanks for calling. Oh, I have some wonderful news for you, but I'll wait until Wednesday night."

"Whatever you say Barbara Walters!" We both laugh.

"Okay honey, see you on Wednesday," I say.

"Natalie, I love you girl."

"Me too."

"Chow!" Renee says quickly and hangs up.

Renee is one of my four sisterfriends. We meet every Wednesday evening for our bonding session. I wouldn't trade my friends for the world. We've been meeting for three years now and I don't think that we could be closer if we were actual blood sisters. Renee Baker is a CPA and the crazy one in the group. She's also the sweetest. She will give you her last dime. Renee is the one to call when you need to talk because she's not judgmental and will always give you honest feedback. Renee is about 5'2", one hundred pounds, short haircut, has skin the color of caramel and these perfect thick lips that so many white women are dying to have.

Lela Lewis is a grant writer and the *'take no shit, I'll curse you out in a minute'* girlfriend. We've been friends since we were thirteen years old. Lela is a healthy woman, about a size fourteen and carries it well. Lela has never been insecure about her size and is so comfortable with herself. I think that's what I liked most about her when we first met. Lela was content with Lela and didn't give a fuck who wasn't. She's down. Lela has big almond shaped eyes with really thick eyebrows. Her skin is brown and reminds me of a chocolate bar. She's a really pretty woman.

Taylor Evansen is the educator. Taylor teaches English at Eldorado High School. Now Taylor is the girlfriend that will be shouting in church on Sunday morning after she had been screwing all Saturday night. "Lord forgive me, but I was horny as hell," she'll say. We all laugh at Taylor because she really does try to live a saved life, but has a weakness just like all of us for big dicks. Taylor is fine. When we are at the gym together the guys don't know which one to approach first. She has a great muscular body, but in a feminine way. Taylor wears her auburn hair shoulder length, usually in braids. A very stylish woman, you'll only catch her wearing the latest designer fashions. Taylor is also the sensitive one in the group, but get her mad and that sensitivity is out the door. She's had some really tough relationships in the past so she has a hard time getting close to men. Taylor starts each of our sessions with a prayer and so we call her The Missionary.

And then there is Naomi Garrett, the *'serious-all-about-business-am-I-set-for-retirement?'* girlfriend. Naomi is from Miami, but moved to Las Vegas about six years ago. We met after she had been here about two months. Naomi can tell you anything you need to know about stocks, bonds, mutual funds, you name it. She works as a financial planner and stays on top of anything that says money. All of our portfolios are in order. Naomi is very conservative and quite selective about who she chooses to associate. It took her a while to warm up to everyone, but now you couldn't tear her apart from us. Naomi is attractive in an Angela Bassett sort of way. Not strikingly beautiful, but has a look that is so unique that men are automatically drawn to her. She can be plain one minute and completely sexy the next. Now, if you ever met Naomi, she would claim that she was shy. That's a bunch of crock. We tell her that her shy game is just a way of reeling men in. They think that they are getting this coy, shy woman and then she pulls out the whips and chains. It is so funny watching her flirt.

I decide to take a bath. I put on a Michael Franks CD and pour some vanilla oil in my bath water. After checking on Pooch, I relax in my roman tub. I allow my mind to drift off and I fall into a deep daze. At first I remember the parking lot scene with Miles and then my mind quickly jumps to last night and I see myself standing in a pool of blood. I immediately snap out of the daze.

I finish bathing and thank God that I do not have to work on weekends. It's my wind down time and gives me time to relax and take it easy. Today I'm going to indulge in a "pamper me day." A PMD day is when I get my hair, nails and feet done. I put on a cute floral sundress by Carole Little and my bright orange Anne Klein sandals. After pinning my hair up and dabbing on some lipstick, I head out the door.

The sky is so incredibly clear and the grass is the purest green I have ever scene. Most people are shocked to see how green the grass is in Las Vegas, considering we're in the middle of the desert. That's the beauty of this place.

CHAPTER 14

I decide to stop at Starbuck's and get a vanilla latte and bagel before heading to the beauty salon. It's crowded as usual. As I'm standing in line I notice a couple sitting at the exact table that Miles and I shared a few nights before. They are smiling at each other and casually flirting. *I wonder if it's their first date?* I start daydreaming of Miles.

"Excuse me, Miss. May I help you?" The young prep behind the counter asks.

"Oh, I'm sorry. My mind is a million miles away."

"That's ok. What can I get you?"

I give her my order and wait a few minutes before my order is ready. I grab a few napkins and a package of cream cheese before heading out of the door. As I'm searching through my purse looking for my keys, I hear a voice.

"Well, well. You had to come back to our spot." It's Miles and he's laughing.

"I can't believe you're here Miles, I was just thinking of you," I say while blushing.

"Something good I hope," he says while leaning towards me and kissing me on the cheek.

"Maybe I'll share it with you later," I say while pulling my keys out.

"Later tonight?" He asks with an interesting look in his eyes.

"Tonight?"

"Yes, tonight?"

"But our date isn't until tomorrow," I say.

"And? What does that have to do with today?"

"I guess nothing but…"

"But what? Do you have plans for tonight?"

"Mmm, I don't know yet. My day is just starting."

"Well, I'd like to see you. That is if you don't mind seeing me two days in a row."

Miles is flirting and I like it.

"How about you call me later on this evening and maybe I'll even cook for you."

"Oh, a lady that's beautiful and can cook." He motions as if he's taking his heart out. "Take my heart now."

""I think that I'll wait on that Mr. Grey. I gotta run. Today is my pamper me day."

"I can do that for you," he says while laughing.

"I bet you can," I say in a sly, sexy way.

Miles opens my car door for me and I slide into my seat.

"I'll talk to you later?"

"Yeah you will," I say.

Miles backs up and closes my door. I wave good-bye and head towards the salon.

CHAPTER 15

Traffic is great this time of day on Spring Mountain Road. This is one of the busiest areas in Las Vegas and I hate being caught in this area around lunch-time because it's a mad house. I pull into the parking lot of Prestige Looks and notice the number of cars. This salon is always booked. One of my girlfriends that I grew up with owns the salon. Sheila Wilson opened Prestige Looks a few years ago and quickly became known as one of the top salons for black women. She and her staff can really do some hair. I walk into the salon and everyone starts clapping. My beautician Debra comes up to me and gives me a big hug and hands be a bouquet of flowers and a card.

"Honey we are so proud of you."

"Thanks Deb, you guys are so sweet."

"How are you feeling Natalie?" yells Sheila as she continues to cut her clients hair.

"I'm fine Sheila. A little overwhelmed, but feeling good."

"Well everyone is just glad that you're safe. Mama said to tell you hello."

"Thanks Sheila, and give Mrs. Wilson my love."

"I will."

I put my things down at Debra's station and meet her at the washbowl. Debra is a great hairdresser. I've been through five hairdressers in the last two years. They're either always late, charge too much, overbooked or don't have a clue about styling hair. I remember when I specifically told this one stylist that I had a sensitive scalp and the perm could not be left on my hair for a long period of time. Did she listen? No! When my scalp started burning, she told me to put my head between my knees and that would stop the burning. Was she out of her mind? And to make matters worse, the salon had run out of hot water and she had to rinse the perm out with cold water. Lord, I had sores on my scalp for days. I couldn't brush my hair for two weeks. Anyway, I am so glad that I found Debra. She is absolutely wonderful.

Deb finishes me up in a little more than an hour and I get my feet and nails done. I'm feeling really good about now. *I think I will cook for Miles.* I chat with Debra for a few minutes and then stop at the grocery store and pick up a few items for *the dinner.*

It's still pretty early when I arrive at home, so I just take my time tidying up my place. I place my flowers in a vase and set them on my dining table. Pooch is busy playing with her beat up bone and appears to be in heaven.

My place is always immaculate and my friends kid me that I'm pretty obsessive when it comes to cleanliness. I've just always liked for things to be in order so if someone just happens to drop by, I'm not throwing things under the bed or in closets trying to neaten up. As I'm walking to my closet to pick out something to wear I notice my answering machine light is blinking.

"I wonder who called?" I say out loud. I check my messages. There are two: One from my Sister Dear and one from my girlfriend Naomi. I better call my Sister Dear back before she curses me out, but first I'll call Miles and let him know that I am definitely cooking.

Day Norwood Williams is my Sister Dear. People are always shocked that we refer to each other as Sister Dear. Well, we just happen to think that we both have the dearest sister in the entire world, and this is how we show our affection. We lost our parents when Day was attending college and I was in junior high school, so she practically raised me. Day is my best friend. She stands 4'11". Let me correct myself: She's 4'11" and a half. She'd kill me if I did not mention the half part. On a good day she wears a size two, and do not tell her that she is not fine. Several years ago she had a bout with anorexia. Yeah, I know what you're thinking. Black girls don't have eating disorders. Yes, they do. I witnessed it firsthand and believe me, it's no joking matter. Day has never gained all of her weight back, but doctors say that she's healthy at 100 pounds. Day is very feisty and fast and loves anything that is tight, short and up her butt. Give her a G-string and a Corona and she's in heaven. Day has beautiful skin, Asian eyes and her trademark gap between her teeth. She keeps her hair cut short and only wears lipstick and blush. Day is married to a wonderful guy, the complete opposite of her. Bryson is very mellow and cool. He reminds me of the singer Seal, his mannerisms and all. They met while attending Tennessee State University and have been together ever since. Day and Bryson live in Virginia with their two sons Gabe and Galen.

I pick up the phone and call Day.

"Hello."

"Hey Sister Dear. It's Nat."

"Hey girl, what's happening?"

"Ah, not much. Just getting ready to cook dinner for my new friend," I say, trying to sound nonchalant.

"You're cooking? Oh shit, who is this man?"

"He's just a friend Day. At least for now!" I laugh.

"Tell me how everything goes cuz if you're cooking for him, you must like him."

"Day, we just started communicating. So far he seems nice. He works at the station with me as a cameraman. His name is Miles."

"Is he fine?"

"He's handsome. He's tall and semi-thick. Clean cut and a smile out of this world."

"Well, he must be nice for you to even give him the time of day, you man-hater!" she says with a laugh.

"Day, I don't hate men, I'm just very untrusting of men."

"Yeah, yeah. Well, go easy on this one ok? Some men can be wonderful if you give them the opportunity."

"I know Sister Dear. I know." Day is always schooling me about my attitude toward men.

"Girl, let me tell you about your brother in law. He is a trip. Last night the boys stayed over our in-laws house and so we had our usual sex-me-up session, right?"

"Yeah."

"Well, I started bleeding a little bit. You know every since I had my surgery I bleed sometimes. The doctor says that it's normal the first few months. Anyway, your crazy brother-in-law says that he's gonna have to stop giving it to me so hard because his dick is just too long and he may be knocking against something."

"Girl, Bryson is a trip," I say chuckling, "Does he think he has a Terminator dick or something?"

"Girl, I don't know, but I laughed so hard I just about died."

"How are my nephews?"

"They're fine, Gabe is playing on his computer and Galeb is sleep. He has a slight cold."

"Tell them hello for me."

Day and I talk for a few more minutes. I tell her about the hostage situation and she nearly has a fit over the telephone. I calm her down and let her know that I'm doing fine. She loved the way Miles approached me, especially the book of poetry. She says that shows his sensitive side. Day says that she will call me tomorrow night for the scoop and to make sure that I wear something sexy, yet feminine for tonight. Something that will make Miles want to eat my pussy on the spot. Day is a wild woman!

I walk to my closet and decide that I'll wear this nice, black jersey, halter dress that flows when I walk. It's fitted, but not too tight. And instead of wearing shoes tonight, I think I'll just go barefoot since we're staying in.

I go into the kitchen and prep all of my food. I'm cooking sautéed mushrooms, Chantilly potatoes, fresh green beans, cucumber salad and broiled steaks. It takes me about an hour to get everything in order. I'll let everything cook slowly while I get dressed. I take a long shower and just lie down on my bed for a little while. The phone rings.

"Hello."

"Natalie, it's Miles."

"Hey you."

"I got your message, but I have to make a stop before I come by, so I'll see you around six-thirty."

"That'll be perfect."

"Ok, I'll see you then."

"Bye."

I'm getting butterflies again, let me calm down.

I walk into the kitchen and check on the food. Everything smells and looks wonderful. I set the table and light about 20 candles throughout my place. I have this passion for candles. I put on some Kenny G and finish getting dressed.

CHAPTER 16

I hear the knock at the door and Pooch is barking like crazy. I take one last look in the mirror. Everything is in place. "Oh, Pooch settle down." I open the door. He's wearing a nice, black linen blend shirt and slacks and some soft black leather espadrilles. His shirt isn't buttoned all the way and a few of his chest hairs are visible. Damn, he looks good!

"Hi Miles, come on in."

"Hey there lady." He walks in. "These are for you."

He hands me a bouquet of beautiful lavender lillies.

"Oh, thanks Miles. That was sweet of you." I smile.

"Anything to make you smile."

"Anything?" I question.

"Anything," he says while reaching into the beige leather wine carrier. "Oh, here's a bottle of wine."

'Why don't you come into the kitchen and pour the wine while I put these in a vase."

"Deal."

Pooch runs up to Miles and sniffs him. *She's not barking, I can't believe it. Usually with strangers she's very unfriendly.*

"Miles this is Pooch, my baby. Pooch this Miles." Miles reaches down and pets Pooch.

"Hey Pooch, nice to meet you. So, this is your baby huh?"

"Yep, the only one," I say.

"How can a brother get this lucky Pooch? Give a brother a clue." Miles rubs Pooch's stomach.

"Pooch, don't give Mommy's secrets away." We both laugh. Pooch runs into the bedroom, I guess she feels as if I'm in good hands.

Miles washes his hands and grabs the dishcloth next to me to dry his hands. I smell him. He smells fresh and clean, almost citrusy. That Calvin Klein smell. Not over-powering, just right.

"So Natalie, how was your day?"

"It was nice Miles. I just pampered me all day and took it easy. It was so pretty outside I hated to come in. I love Vegas this time of year."

"Me too, it's great."

He grabs the wine glasses from the table and pours the wine. I watch him pour the wine. I watch how he moves, how his clothes hang on his body just right.

"You have a nice place here. I like the way you've decorated. I take it black, cream and mauve are your favorite colors?"

"You got it right." We both smile. I can tell that we're both still a little nervous.

I check the food one last time and put everything on low.

"Miles the food will be ready in just a few minutes okay?"

"That's cool. I'm not really hungry right now even though what you're cooking smells great. I'd like to just sit with you for a while and talk."

"That'll be fine. Let's have a seat in here." We walk into the living room and sit on the sofa. It looks really nice and romantic with the candles flickering all over and the scent of vanilla drifting in the air.

Miles hands me a glass of wine. "What shall we toast to?" he asks.

"To new friends." I say.

"To new friends." We toast.

"Have I told you how nice you look?" He gives me that piercing look again.

"No you haven't," I say while blushing.

"Well, you look beautiful."

"Thank you. Miles are you nervous?"

"Are you nervous Nat?"

"A little bit. I've had butterflies all day thinking about seeing you tonight," he says.

"I can't believe Mr. Grey would be nervous about a date."

"Not just a date," he says slowly. "But time with you."

Miles puts his glass of wine down and grabs mine from my hand. He stands up and pulls me up close to him as he takes my face in his hands gently and says, "This may be a little forward of me, but I've been thinking about kissing you all day."

Miles kisses my forehead, my nose, my cheek and my chin softly. *I'm melting again.* Then he brushes his lips against mine almost like a soft breeze. He gently licks my lips as if he's savoring the taste. His lips are thick and soft. His hands are still on my face. He slides his tongue into my mouth and runs it across my teeth, *s l o w l y*, and then he kisses me. I taste him for the first time. He taste good. His mouth is hot and next to mine it's sweltering. He explores my mouth while teasing my tongue and then he kisses me really hard and deep. *God, I'm going crazy!* I reach up and wrap my arms around his neck and let my fingers gently massage the nap of his neck. Miles is holding me tight. Our chests are touching and I can feel his penis growing bigger and harder. He stops.

"Let me see your body Natalie. Take your dress off." Miles takes his finger and traces my shoulder. *I'm breathless. My coochie is wet as hell. Shit! I don't know what's wrong with me, but I don't say a word. I just oblige him.*

I slip out of my dress and stand in only my G-string. Miles sits on the couch and leans back. "Come here," he says as takes my hands and pulls me towards him. I mount him and he just looks at me for a moment. He shakes his head and whispers, "Damn, you're beautiful. I just want to touch you and kiss you and make you feel good."

"Listen Miles, I've never been in a situation like this so quick. This is not common for me and I can't just jump into bed with you. I'm sure you're thinking why am I nearly naked on top of you."

"Shhh. Natalie, I know what type of woman you are. You don't have to explain anything to me. I'm not trying to get you into bed. At least not tonight." He smiles. "I just want to make you feel good. Let me explore your body."

Miles pulls me against him and kisses me hard and passionately. I feel his hands on my breasts, my back, my butt. Everywhere. He lays me on the couch and kneels beside me.

"You're so soft," he says and he gently kisses my breasts. My nipples are hard and my body burns with desire. He takes his tongue and makes a trail to my naval where he plays for awhile. His hand barely touches the crotch of my panties and sends chills through me. I feel his mouth searching my inner thighs. He spreads my legs and runs his tongue across my paradise. I moan and arch my back. Miles removes my panties and kneels between my legs while removing his shirt. I feel his fingers parting the lips of my paradise and then he inserts one of his fingers and finds the spot. *I'm dying.*

"Oh Miles, that feels good, please don't stop!"

"I won't baby, this is for you." He inserts another finger and works the "G" until I can't take it anymore. He puts one of his fingers in his mouth and sucks it. "Mmmm, you taste good." His voice changes to a deep sensuous tone. He puts the other finger in my mouth. I suck his finger slowly and watch how it turns him on.

Lord Jesus, this is too much. Miles spreads my heaven and I can feel the heat of his breath against my passion and I'm lost in pleasure. I grab his head and press it between my thighs. I can feel his tongue discovering the inner depths of my wet walls. He then gently takes his tongue and flicks across my clit back and forth. I shudder in ecstasy as he sucks softly. I run my hands across his shoulders and back. His body is hard and smooth. The more he sucks the louder my moans become. He then puts his tongue deep inside of me. "Oh God!" I scream. "I'm coming Miles."

"Take your time sweetheart," he says. Miles plays my symphony until it flows like a river. I'm limp and loving it. He lifts me up to him and we kiss.

"Now that's what I call an appetizer," he whispers in my ear.

"You're crazy Miles."

"Just over you girl. Just over you." We hold each other for several minutes and savor the moment while the music plays softly. His head is on my chest. I caress his face.

"Miles that was really nice," I whisper.

"Yeah, it was. I could eat you all night. Literally."

"We'll have to try that one night." We laugh.

"Only if you can handle it," he says while smiling.

"We'll see Mr. Grey. Now let's eat. I'm starving."

"Me too."

We decide to sit out on the patio and enjoy the wonderful dinner that I prepared. The sky is so clear and the stars seem to be shining a bit brighter tonight. I wonder why? Miles and I discuss what we want and desire in a relationship. Our hopes and dreams. Sports. Politics. Everything. Before we know it, it's 2a.m.

"Natalie, I had a wonderful time. You're a special woman and not to mention a great cook!"

"Thanks Miles. I had a great time too. I can't believe it's so late. Time just flew by."

"Are we still on for church?"

"Yes we are, 8 a.m. sharp," I say.

"I'll be here at 7:45."

"Good, I like a man who's prompt."

"And I like a woman like you." Miles walks around the table and pulls me up from my seat. He kisses me. "You feel so good in my arms lady."

"Likewise," I say in his ear.

"I better go, see you in the morning."

"Okay." I walk Miles to the front door and we steal another kiss. "Call me when you get home."

"I will." I watch him as he gets in his Jeep. I close the door.

I'm floating.

CHAPTER 17

He arrives promptly at 7:45 a.m. on the dot. He's wearing a nice, single- breasted Brioni suit in slate blue with a cream dress shirt with thin, barely visible slate blue lines, along with a matching silk tie. He looks extremely handsome. "Good morning Miles." I say as I take in every inch of him. "Good morning beautiful," he says while gently pulling me close to him and softly kissing my lips. "Are you ready?" he asks.

"For what?" I ask.

"Church of course. What else?" he says while laughing.

"Yes I am, just let me grab my purse."

We both say goodbye to Pooch and head to church. As usual Second Baptist is crowded. Eight o'clock service is normally packed. That's because it starts at eight and you're out the door by nine-thirty. Perfect. None of that hour-long-testifying-session-same-people- every-Sunday-shouting-look-who's-wearing–what-those-who-will-give

-$20-stand-versus-those-who-will-give-ten-dollars-stand-missionary- gossiping-all-day-preaching-about- nothing-crap…and by the time you leave church it's 4p.m. No Lord, give me eight o'clock service any day.

The choir is excellent today and Reverend Davis gives an excellent sermon on family responsibility. Miles stands and introduces himself during the welcoming of the guests. Man Alert! Man Alert! The sisters were looking at him like he was a piece of Popeye's fried chicken and breaking their neck to see whom he was with. These women are a trip. After benediction we're heading out the door and I could not keep track of how many sisters ran up to us welcoming Miles and inviting him back. "Miles is it? Oh welcome to our church. Would you be interested in joining our bible study class? Please, please do come back again." He handled it well. Holding my hand the entire time and responding with, "Well, if Natalie invites me back, I'll be back." I liked that and they got the message really quick: His attention and focus is on the woman he is with. We finally make our way to the car.

"Natalie, church service was really nice."

"Yeah, Reverend Davis really preached today."

"He made some really interesting points about family. I really liked his views on mentoring. We really do need more people taking an interest in those kids who don't have parents to guide them or positive role models."

"This is true. That's why I spend so much time with the girls at the youth center. So many of them need guidance and attention."

"Yeah, I know what you mean."

"So Miles, what would you like to do today?" I ask.

"Well, let's get a bite to eat and then we can change clothes and catch a matinee."

"Sounds good."

We decide to have brunch at Marie Callender's. I order pancakes, eggs and hash browns and he orders a Mexican omelette. We end up eating off of each other's plate while talking and laughing the entire time. There's not a dull moment in our conversation, it just goes smoothly from one subject to the next. It's easy talking to Miles. He really listens and takes a sincere interest in what I'm saying.

"Two days in row. I can't believe it," Miles says while shaking his head.

"Why can't you believe it?" I ask.

"I just can't believe that you would allow me to be in your presence Miss Thang, considering how you were when we first went out. Man, I thought you hated men."

"Miles, you sound like my sister. I don't hate men. I just haven't had the best relationships and for the most part I don't trust men. It may sound crude, but that's just how I feel."

"Well, I'll just have to work on that with you." He pauses. "That is if you let me."

"I'll think about it Miles."

"Good, at least a brother got you thinking about it." He smiles. We both laugh.

Miles had a change of clothes, so we go back to my place before heading to the movies. He goes into the bathroom and changes while I change in my bedroom. The telephone rings.

"Hello."

"Hi gorgeous." I freeze in place. I haven't heard this voice in four years. *Why is he calling me? How did he get my number? Shit!*

"Hello Derrick." My voice is clipped with irritation. "To what do I owe this phone call?"

"I'm just calling to say hello and to see how my one true love is doing."

"I'm doing wonderful Derrick. Now what do you really want?"

"Baby, I want to see you, " he says in that same tone that used to get to me and is getting to me now.

"No! You cannot see me Derrick and do not call me again. Do you hear me? You caused me enough grief. Stay the fuck out my life!"

I hang up the phone and turn my answering machine on. My head is pounding. How dare he call me? Who does he think he is? Calling me after four years to say he wants to see me? I can't believe this. My stomach is flipping.

Derrick Foster is, well, was my college sweetheart. God I loved that man! I slept with his sweater every night for three years. All he had to do was say jump and I'd ask, "How high?" I loved that man's stanky drawers. Stayed up all night typing his homework while he slept or got high. Kept his apartment spotless. Cooked him dinner every night. Fucked him at the drop of a dime. Just crazy stupid over this thin -ass man who happened to be the campus whore. And now what? He calls and disrupts my emotions. Well not today.

My phone rings again. I don't answer it. I sit on my bed and put my head in hands. I can feel my veins about to explode. Why am I letting this man get to me after all these years?

"Are you ok Natalie?"

Damn, I forgot Miles was here.

"Oh Miles, yeah I'm ok."

"You don't sound ok. Whoever that was on the phone really upset you." He sits next to me and wraps his arms around me.

"Really Miles, I'm ok…let's just continuing having a wonderful day." I try to sound encouraging, but I know my feelings show on my face and in my voice.

"Alright, but you better put some clothes on first." He's smiling.

I look down, I only have on my bra and panties. "Oh! I didn't real…."

"Hey, I definitely don't mind."

"Miles you are silly. I'll be ready in a sec." I walk toward my closet, I can feel his eyes on me. Thank goodness for Victoria's Secret. I have on this silk set in a beautiful shade of coral. I know he's dying 'cuz the butt is tight! I put on a pair of khaki shorts, a chambray shirt and some loafers. "I'm ready."

"Then let's go." he says. We take his Jeep this time. He has some Boys II Men playing softly.

"So, are you going to tell me about this mystery phone call or do I have to force it out of you." he asks in a warm manner not pushy.

"It's nothing Miles," I say while looking out the window.

"Well, for you to tell someone to stay out of your fuckin life," he says while raising his hands slightly off the steering wheel, "it has to be something?"

"It's my ex-boyfriend Miles. He wants to see me and I do not want to see him. End of story."

"Are you sure?" he probes with a tad bit of doubt in his voice.

"I'm positive."

"Then I'll leave it alone," he says while taking my hand in his. *Am I sure I'm positive? Hell no, but I can't show him that. Smile and have a great time at the movies.*

CHAPTER 18

I get home around 8:30. Pooch greets me at the door in her usual perky way. As I'm walking into my bedroom, I notice that my answering machine light is blinking like crazy. "Gee, how many people have called me today?" I play back all the messages, 12 total. Five of the messages are from Derrick. I feel sick. I need to talk to someone, so I call Renee.

"Hello."

"Hey Chick. It's me!" I say trying not to sound too pitiful.

"Hey Nat, what's wrong? You don't sound like yourself."

"Girl, Derrick called and he wants to see me."

"Shut up! Derrick love- hang-over Derrick?" She's laughing.

I start laughing. "Renee this is serious girl. I can't be talking to that man. He is nothing but trouble and heartache with a capital H."

"Oh, come on Nat. That was four years ago, he's probably changed."

"Chile please! If Derrick has changed, Michael Jackson has his original nose!"

We both burst into laughter.

"Nat you are wild girl. But seriously, people do change. You and Derrick were both very young and naive. Plus he had nearly every babe on campus throwing pussy in his face just because he was an Omega man. What's a brother to do? Just say no? I don't think so. I think you're being too hard on him."

"Well Renee, I hear you, but I'm just not ready to see him. Even after four years my stomach gets knotted just thinking about him. I just can't do it."

"Sweetie, don't do anything that makes you uncomfortable. But you'll have to talk to him sooner or later. You know how persistent he can be."

"Then it will have to be later." I reply. "I can't deal with him right now. Anyhow, my interest is elsewhere."

"Oh yeah, I forgot! Mr. Miles. Taylor told me about this new interest. How's that going?"

"I cooked for him last night and today he went to church with me."

"And, what else?" Renee knows me too well.

"What do you mean Renee?" I ask shyly.

"Girl, give it up. It's me you're talking to." We laugh. I give Renee a blow by blow of what took place last night. Especially the part about Miles just wanting to please me.

She could not handle it. She says that I am too wild for her and wanted to know if Miles had a brother. We talk for about two hours and before hanging up she reminds me that we're meeting at Lela's on Wednesday night for our Sisterfriends session.

I decide to just chill in silence for a moment before I shower and get ready for bed. I had a really nice time with Miles, he's so sweet and considerate and refreshing. I think I can sorta kinda like him. I laugh to myself considering my thoughts on the male species. But Miles seems different. More mature, more focused, more sensitive…just more. As I'm having fun recapturing all of yesterday and today my phone rings. I pick up.

"Good evening." I say.

"That I did have." A sexy voice replies. It's Miles.

"Hi there." Immediately, I feel fluttery inside.

"Did I catch you at a bad time?" He asks.

"No, I was just lying on my bed relaxing for a moment."

"Well, I just wanted to thank you for a lovely weekend, and I hope we can do it again."

"It would be my pleasure Miles. We'll do it again very soon." I say.

"How soon?" he quickly asks.

"Soon."

"Tonight?" he says with a chuckle.

"No Miles, not tonight. But maybe tomorrow after work."

"A brother will take what he can get." We laugh.

"Sleep well beautiful, I'll talk to you later."

"Goodnight Miles."

We hang up and I allow myself to continue feeling this happy for a few more moments before jumping in the shower. I decide to try my new raspberry bath gel. It smells wonderful. I take my time bathing. It dawns on me that tomorrow I have a meeting with Frank Holmes, the general manager of the station. After showering, I select a nice Calvin Klein power suit to wear for the big meeting. I say my prayers and thank God for emotional peace.

I'm not sleep for long when my phone rings. I look over at my clock, it's 12:05. Who the hell is calling me at this hour? It had better be an emergency. "Hello, and what is so important that you had to wake me at this time of night?"

The voice on the other end replies, "I'm sorry I woke you, but I need to talk to you baby. Please don't hang up." *Damn it! It's Derrick. Do I hang up? Damn! Damn! Damn!*

"First of all, you did wake me and I'm beat. Secondly, I am *not* your baby."

"I'm sorry Nat okay, I'm sorry," he says pathetically.

"What is it Derrick? What do you want?"

"I just want to talk to you, that's all. Just talk."

"Derrick, what is there to talk about? Let's see. Should we talk about you and Kyla or you and Tasha? Or should we talk about you screwing another woman in your living room while I was asleep in your bedroom? Or should we talk about you standing me up for the holidays because you said that you had the flu, but you were actually spending Christmas with Stephanie in Arizona. Or…"

"Okay Nat I get it."

"No Derrick you don't get it. That's the whole point, you never got it! Now after four fucking years, lightening has struck your yellow ass? Fuck you Derrick. I've wanted to say that to you for a long time, but I couldn't bring myself to say anything harsh to you because I loved you. But you listen and listen hard: You cold, heartless, insensitive, unrefined asshole! Love don't fuckin live here anymore!" I hang up the phone and turn my ringer off. I'm so pissed that I'm boiling. I start crying because I feel all the pain that this man caused me for years. Years that I let him abuse my heart. I'm crying because even though he put me through hell, there's a part of me that still loves him and that pisses me off. *Why can't I hate him? God help me!* I know that eventually I'll have to talk to him because like Renee said he's persistent as hell, but we'll talk when I say so and right now is not the time.

I get out of bed and fix a cup of herb tea. As I'm adding the honey and lemon I try to relax. Pooch has followed me into the kitchen. I give her a few snacks and decide to sit at the dining table for a few. The hot tea calms my nerves. The tension in my temples starts to leave. *I can handle this.* I take a deep breath, rest my head on the table and mentally visualize myself on a beach somewhere in the Caribbean. A few moments later I'm relaxed. I climb back into bed and let my mind drift back to the previous nights romantic interlude. I think of kissing Miles, of holding him, and somewhere in the midst of the sweltering thought, I fall asleep.

CHAPTER 19

It's Monday morning and I'm watching the sun seep through my mini-blinds. I lie in my bed in complete tranquility. Quietness takes over my mind. My inner spirit is at peace. I hear birds begin to sing. I listen closely. I feel as if I can hear the world awakening and opening its eyes at God's command. I stretch my arms wide and realize that I too am part of this daily ritual, this rebirth. I am truly blessed.

I cannot believe how well rested I feel, considering how much I tossed and turned last night after Derrick's call.

Life is a trip! One minute you're having a fucking orgasm and damn near floating on Mars and the next you're having hemorrhoids the size of golf balls! Go figure! After saying my morning prayer, I head to the gym. I'm shocked to see Naomi with Taylor. Naomi is not a morning person. How in the world did Taylor manage to get her here?

"Hey sweeties! What's happening?" I ask as I walk towards them.

"Nothing much girl, just tired as hell. I had a rough night." Naomi says.

"Girl, I know the feeling. Did Taylor tell you that Derrick called?"

"Yeah, I couldn't believe it Nat. Why now?"

"Who knows Naomi? All I know is that I can't deal with him right now and just thinking about the whole thing makes me sick."

"Girl, don't get your panties all up your butt because of Derrick. Listen here, he's coming to you now and he's in your territory. Don't sweat this shit. Let his ass sweat, and when you're ready to talk to him and only when you're ready then you decide when and where," says Taylor in her usual sassy way.

"I hear ya, but I'm still a little nervous. That man does something to me!"

"Nat, Taylor is right. He's in your ball park now. You guys are not in college and he's not dealing with an 18-year-old girl. You're a woman now, and he has to come correct or not at all."

"I agree with everything you're both saying. I've said the exact same thing a thousand times in my mind ever since he called, but my damn heart keeps trippin remembering stuff!"

"You'll be alright," Naomi says while hugging me. "Shit, he'll be eating out of your hand this time. Don't you worry about a thing. He ain't met this new diva!

We all laugh. "I hope you're right, cuz I can't be trippin with Derrick again," I say.

Our workout is great. Naomi decides she'll start meeting us at the gym every morning. Now all we have to do is convince Lela. I can hear Lela now, "Fuck no, I ain't waking up at no goddamn five-o'clock to jump around with you skinny heifers!"

We'd all bust out laughing. Lela is a trip.

I arrive at the store around a quarter to 10 and before I walk inside I feel something eerie. Something gloomy. I've always been able to sense something bad. Even as a small child I remember knowing something bad was about to take place before it happened. As I approach the door, I hesitate for a moment. "Natalie, you're getting too sensitive." I say out loud. I walk in the store, and it's obvious that something is wrong. My employees are crying.

Sally is walking towards me. Her eyes are bloodshot red.

"Sally, honey what's wrong?"

"Oh Natalie!" Sally plunges into my arms. I hold her tightly.

"I can't believe, I just can't believe it!," she yells hysterically.

"Sally, calm down and tell me what's wrong," I say as I grab hold of her shoulders and start wiping tears from her eyes.

"He's dead Natalie. He's dead!"

"Who's dead?" I ask. Fear creeps inside of me.

She looks at me for moment and tries to speak, but can't. "Take your time Sally and tell me who died."

"It's Jay," she says softly, "he's dead."

I can't believe my ears.

"Did you say that Jay is dead? When? How?" I'm hysterical now.

"This morning. His mom found him in his apartment."

"Oh my God, Sally. Jesus, I can't believe this. Just a few days ago we were kidding around. What happened?"

"Apparently, Jay has been sick for a while."

"Sick. When? For how long?" I try to take all of this in.

"For a long time. He swore his mother to secrecy."

"His mother? How is she doing?"

"She's doing okay, she's been preparing herself for this for some time now, so she's handling it quite well."

"I cannot believe this. Do we know when the arrangements are?" I ask.

"Yeah, they're Thursday morning at Palm."

"Okay, I'll take care of everything on our part." We both stand in the middle of the aisle and cry. Customers walk and stare at us. We realize that we need to take this conversation off the floor. I open my office door and we sit on the sofa.

"Sally?" My voice quivers and I try to gain my composure.

"Yes, Nat," she says while reaching for a Kleenex. Sally wipes her eyes and takes a deep breath. I notice that she is clenching her hands tightly. They are starting to turn red. I'm sure it's her nerves.

"Did you know that Jay was sick?"

"Not really, but I suspected it. Didn't you notice his weight loss? He was living his life too carelessly and he didn't fear getting AIDS. I guess that's because he was already living with it."

Sally is devastated; she and Jay were so close.

"Listen, why don't you take the day off. I can handle everything around here."

"Thanks Nat, you're so kind."

"Don't mention it," I say. We hug tightly. "Go home, I'll call you later."

Sally leaves and I cry in silence. I realize that I did not care for the way Jay handled his business, but he was a nice guy and a hard worker. I'll miss him calling me Miss Thang and imitating Diana Ross. I smile and say a prayer for Jay and his loved ones.

I decide to get off the couch and tackle the paper work on my desk, but first I call the florist and order an arrangement of sunflowers to be sent to Jay's mom.

Sunflowers were Jay's favorite flower. Once a month he bought an arrangement to sit on his desk. He always joked that sunflowers were bright and lovely like him.

I type a memo to the staff informing them of the tragedy and ask those who wish to attend the funeral to let me know by tomorrow evening. Finally, I call our store across town requesting staff coverage for Thursday morning.

"I need coffee," I think as I head over to the kitchenette and put on some fresh ground vanilla-nut coffee. I lean against the counter and massage my temples. Just when I'm about to relax and my nerves are calming down, there's a knock at the door. "Come in," I say, trying not to sound annoyed or bothered. It's Kimberly, one of my salesgirls.

"Miss Natalie, sorry to disturb you, but there's a delivery for you." Kimberly is so cute. She has this Southern accent that'll knock you off your feet. She is the epitome of a Southern Belle.

"A delivery? What is it?" I ask.

"I think you better come out here and see for yourself." Kimberly has this mischievous look on her face and I'm looking at her like, "What are you about to show me that I'm not going to like?"

I follow Kimberly out of my office and am shocked at what's before my eyes. Flowers. Every shade. Every size. Every color. Roses. Tulips. Lilies. Carnations. Violets. Gardenias. Flowers everywhere. I can't believe what I'm seeing. "What's going on?" I ask trying to figure out who would send all of these flowers.

"I don't know, but whoever he is I want to meet him!," Kimberly says. "Oh, I almost forgot. This is the card that came with the flowers."

Kimberly hands me the card. I open the tiny envelope slowly. *One flower couldn't capture your beauty nor the love I have in my heart for you. Derrick…P.S Please call me 658-8262.*

I'm numb. First Jay and now Derrick. *How am I suppose to deal with all of this emotion?* "Thanks Kim."

"Gee, someone loves you darlin'."

"Yeah," I say in a daze.

"What do you want us to do with all of these?" She asks while pointing to my garden.

"Oh, tell the staff to help themselves. I'll send whatever is left to the church."

"That's very generous of you Natalie, but at least take these yellow roses into your office." Kimberly hands me the lovely bouquet. "Thanks Kim."

I walk into my office, quickly pour a cup of coffee and tackle my paperwork. No way am I going to allow my mind to think about this Derrick situation right now.

CHAPTER 20

"Hello Mr. Holmes."

"Frank, please." We shake hands and smile. Frank is dressed in a sharp navy suit with burgandy accessories. He has an athletic built and has kept himself well to be in his early 50's. The gray hints around his temples. It's obvious that back in his day he was fine. He pulls out one of the chairs in front of his desk for me to sit down. His office is decorated nicely in cherry wood and deep cherry leather. The wall behind his desk holds several plaques and awards for broadcasting. There is a large picture of him and his family among the awards.

"Natalie, thanks for coming. Would you like something to drink? Coffee? Juice? Water?"

"No thank you Frank, I'm fine."

"That you are. No pun intended. And no, I'm not flirting. I just think it's necessary to give a compliment when it's deserved." He smiles, sits in his chair and leans back.

"Well, thank you for the compliment and to answer your question, no, I wouldn't like anything to drink." I smile. *Yeah, sure you're not flirting. And my name is Whitney Houston.*

"Natalie, the station is very proud of you. You put your life on the line and that took a lot of courage."

"I was just doing my job Frank. Any reporter in my shoes would have done the same thing," I say trying to sound modest.

"No Natalie, I beg to differ. The average reporter never would have gone in. No buddy! You are by no means an average reporter, " Frank says while shaking his head.

"I wanted to do a good job and I didn't want any more lives lost." I explain as my nervousness leaves and comfort settles in. I sink deeper in my chair.

"Well, we're glad that you were able to reach that young man. The story got national attention. You're famous young lady!" Frank is excited.

"Famous? Uh, I wouldn't go that far," I say with a chuckle.

Frank leans forward, "I don't think you realize how big this story was. We have arranged for you to be interviewed by "Dateline" This is really big!"

Man, he was really serious when he called me. Part of me thought that this couldn't be true.

"When is the interview?" I ask.

"Wednesday morning," he says excitedly. "Which brings me to why I asked for this meeting." Frank pauses and gets this serious look on his face. His forehead wrinkles slightly between his eyebrows. *Oh, my god...what is it?* "What would you think about a full-time position here?"

Did I just hear this man correctly? Did he just ask me if I wanted a full-time position here? Shit, I have to be dreaming.

"A full-time position?" I ask. I need to hear this again.

"Yes. As you probably already know we're about to expand our newscast to include a mid-day report. We've already hired a gentleman out of Dallas and we think you two would make a perfect team."

"I can't believe this! An anchor position? Frank, I've never anchored before and...

"Listen Natalie, don't worry," he cuts me off. "We have eight weeks before the first broadcast. We'll have you ready in no time. Besides, we have all the confidence in the world that you'll do a fine job." Frank is obviously just as excited as I am if not more.

"Well, what can I say?"

"Yes, would be nice."

"By all means, yes! Yes, I accept*!" I cannot believe that this is happening to me. I feel like jumping up and down, but I keep my composure, as much as I can.*

"Good, you've made an excellent decision. You're well on your way kid!" Frank stands up and extends his hand towards me. "Virginia, my secretary will go over everything with you in the morning and get your paperwork together."

"Thank you so much Mr. Holmes. This is a wonderful opportunity and I won't let the station down."

"No, thank you. The station is lucky to have you on our team."

Frank walks me to the door and we say goodbye. I know I am grinning like Chester Cheese. I walk outside the building. I need air.

"Ahhhhhhhhhhhhhhh!!!! Thank you God!" I scream and do a little dance in the parking lot.

Unbeknownst to me, Miles is standing outside watching my whole reaction.

"Good news I take it?" he asks

I'm startled. "Oh, it's you!" My shock quickly turns to pleasure once I see his face.

"Yes, it's me. Now what has you so excited pretty lady?"

"Oh Miles, you are never going to believe what just happened! I mean I can't believe it!"

"Slow up, take a deep breath and tell me," Miles says.

"Okay, I just left a meeting with Frank Holmes."

"And?"

"And he just offered me the noon anchor position!"

"Oh Nat, that is great! I am so proud of you!" Miles reaches towards me and gives me a big hug and kiss on the cheek. I love how his arms feel around me.

"Thanks Miles. I am so happy I don't know what to do."

"I knew something was going on today. When I got to work, the newsroom was buzzing about who was going to get the new position. Everyone's going to be shocked, huh?"

He smiles at me.

"Yeah they are." I say.

"Hey, but who cares? As far as I'm concerned, you are the best choice by far."

"Aren't you being a little biased Miles?"

"Of course I am. And is anything wrong with me having good taste?"

"No, not at all. Not at all." I reach for him and kiss his lips softly. "Thank you," I whisper in his ear. "I never could have done this without you. I owe you."

"When can I collect?" He asks slyly.

"Soon, very soon," I say. I kiss him again, only this time I put a little something on his mind.

CHAPTER 21

It's Wednesday night and we're all meeting at Taylor's house for our monthly sisterfriends session. We all pull up to the house within seconds on of each other. Renee yells out to everyone, "Hey babes, what's shakin?" Renee has a new haircut and hair color. It's sort of bronzy. It goes great with her golden complexion.

"Girl ain't nothin goin on but the rent and crazy white folks!" Lela says. We all laugh. "I like your hair Renee, it's really cute," says Naomi.

"Thanks Naomi, I needed a change," Renee says.

"How's everyone?" I ask.

Everyone says they're fine.

"How are you Superwoman?" Renee asks.

"I'm great, I have some wonderful news to share tonight."

"Good, I need some," Lela interjects.

We walk towards the door and Naomi rings the doorbell. Taylor answers the door wearing the cutest yellow sundress.

"Come on in y'all. I ordered us some Chinese food and the wine is chilling."

Taylor has a really nice place. She is very much into aromatherapy and atmosphere. There are candles and potpourri everywhere and a cd of nature sounds plays on the stereo. Beautiful African prints cover her walls along with shelves adorned with African figures. There is no living room furniture in Taylor's home, just lots of big decorative pillows that surround a hand-carved table. Taylor says that when people come to her home, they have to sit on the floor and that sitting on the floor removes their egos and allows them to connect with their true selves. So far, it's worked for us. We each find our place around the table and fill our wine glasses.

"To friendship, love and happiness. Today, tomorrow and always," we say in unison. We lift our glasses and toast.

"So, where did we end off last time?" Taylor asks.

"We discussed Naomi venturing out and starting her own business; Lela leaving Joe until he grows up; Renee's miscarriage; You having sex with men too quick, and me hating men." I say.

We all start laughing. "Girl, you are crazy!" Taylor says.

"I know, I can't help myself. Well, who wants to start off the meeting?"

"I will," says Naomi. "I applied for a small business loan and the loan officer said that it was very rare that she ever came across paperwork so thoroughly prepared. She said that she often had to send people back to re-do this and that, but that my stuff was together. Thanks to my sisterfriends of course." We all clap.

"That's wonderful Naomi! So, how soon will they let you know?" Lela asks.

"I should know within a few weeks and then its hello Naomi and Associates."

"I know that's right," says Taylor.

"Well, I had lunch with Ty and officially broke things off. I told him that I was ready for a commitment and he obviously wasn't. Therefore, I had to move on. He pulled that, 'I love you more than life crap', but this time I stood firm. I really love Ty, but he isn't ready to settle down. How long am I suppose to wait for him?"

"Girl, you're not! All of that negative energy and vibe could be keeping your real prince charming away. Out with the old and in with the new!" Taylor says in her usual perky way. Everyone nods in agreement.

Renee speaks next. "I'm feeling better about my miscarriage. At first I was really depressed because I really wanted this baby, but I realize that things happen for a reason. Shit, I'm not married. Tony and I are at each other's throat every other day and I had to ask myself was I really prepared to bring a child into this world. The answer was no. Now don't get me wrong, there's still a part of me that aches when I think about it, but overall I'm much better."

"We're glad that you're feeling better Renee. We all knew it would just take some time for you to heal," I say.

"I haven't screwed in three weeks and it's been a killer on T.O.M.!" Taylor says. We die laughing. "Who is Tom?" We ask in unison. "Oh you guys know T.O.M: Time Out for Masturbation. My dildo sillies!" We fall back in laughter. Each of us cry from laughing so hard. Taylor is a trip. We gain our composure and Lela says, "Well Miss Nat, when are you going to fill us in on Mr. Cameraman?"

"Yeah girl, I heard," interjects Naomi.

"Alright, alright."

Just as I'm about to start, the doorbell rings. It's our Chinese food. As we're eating I tell my sisterfriends about Miles and the re-appearance of Derrick.

"Well, I think you should give this Miles guy a try. What do you have to lose?" Renee asks.

"Naw, this Miles guy sounds too good to be true. Any man that eats your pussy and then sets it on chill for the night is trouble with a capital T." Naomi interjects while reaching for some chips.

"I agree with Renee." Lela says. "You've been by your-self long enough. Your damn pussy is old and damn near on Medicare. If this Miles guy is treating you nice and making you feel good, I say go for it!"

Taylor lends her advice: "I think you should meet with Derrick. You really loved him, and from the sound of things, you've never really gotten over him. Meet with him and see where he's coming from. Don't open the door for Miles until you've closed it completely with Derrick."

"Derrick wasn't shit when you met him and I'd bet all I have that that niggah ain't shit now!" Lela shouts.

"Lela, that was while they were in college. They were both babies." Renee says.

"Babies or no babies. His yellow ass was a dog then and dogs never change!" Lela's anger is quite apparent and catches everyone, including me, off guard.

"Come on Lela, people do change." I say.

"I don't think so," Lela says sarcastically.

"Thanks you guys. You've really made this easy for me. I really like Miles and I'd love to see more of him however, there's a part of me that has never gotten over Derrick

What Naomi said is true. Derrick and I were babies when we first got involved and that was years ago. We're both adults now."

"Why are you being so stupid?" Lela shouts. "Damn I can't believe I am hearing this. You damn near flunked outta college over this fool and now just because a few years have passed, you want to give him another try. Stupid."

"Hold up Lela!" Renee says forcefully. "Where do you get off calling Natalie stupid? Do we need to remind you about Joe? Joe, a man that has beat you, screwed your cousin, got credit cards in your name and put you ten thousand dollars in debt. A man that isn't worth 10 cents, yet you have taken him back a thousand times and each time we stood by your decision even though we each gritted our teeth. No, we didn't like your decision, but we wanted you to be happy. Neither of us have ever called you stupid and I think you are out of line!"

"Well, excuse the fuck outta me!"

"Lela, don't go there!" Taylor cautions.

"No!" she says waving her hands. "I'm just trying to help her ass!"

"No Lela, you're just being your usual self. Pointing out faults in everyone else, yet quickly forgetting the things you've gone through," I say as I take a sip of wine and try to stay calm.

"That's right Lela. Why do you always pick apart everybody's relationship and then if either of us say one thing about Joe, you have a fit?" Naomi asks.

"Ain't this some shit?" Lela asks while rolling her eyes. "Is this jump on Lela night?"

"No Lela it's not," Renee says as she touches Lela's arm. "We've talked to you before on how you say things and how quick you are to judge our lives and not your own."

"Well, next time I'll just keep my mouth shut." Lela crosses her arms and sucks her teeth in disgust.

"Oh, grow up Lela. We're giving you constructive criticism. Take it, ponder over it and go on. Why do we have to have so much drama from you when you are clearly in the wrong. The drama is getting old!" *I have just about had it with Lela. She pulls this crap every time she is put on the spot about how she talks to us. I'm sick of her attitude.*

"Okay Lela." Taylor says in a very calming tone. "You are wrong. Period. All you had to do was apologize to Natalie for calling her stupid. There is a way to voice your feelings without being rude and hurtful. What you said to Natalie was wrong."

"I'm sorry you guys," Lela says with a gentle tone. "I'm sorry Natalie. It's just that I am so stressed out over Joe. I can't live with him and I can't live without him. What am I supposed to do now?"

"That's it, you're basing your whole happiness and being on this man. How many times have we all told you that your happiness has to come from within?" says Naomi.

"Joe does exactly what you allow him to do. You've never really put your foot down with him. It's just like me and sex. The minute I stopped jumpin' in bed with these fools, I got some respect and things changed," Taylor says.

"You have let Joe get away with so much, and now you want him to be someone completely new. Like I've always said, 'set the rules in the beginning and stick to them'," Renee says and snaps her fingers.

My anger is leaving and I finally say something, "Lela, we all know how much you love Joe and I am sure that he loves you in his own way, but is hurting like this every month worth it? Joe has lost all respect for you. You know it, I know it, we all know it. But there's one thing for sure: Lela has got to love and respect Lela. If Lela doesn't, who will?"

Lela cries and we each feel her pain because we've all been there. All of us have been in a relationship that took every ounce of our being and each of us kept trying to fix it and make it work, but it never happened. Then one day we woke up and said no more, and that's what Lela has to do and mean it.

"I hear each of you, but I've been with this man for eight years. How do I just start over?"

"One day at a time Lela," Naomi says. "You know how I was after I broke up with William. Shit, I was devastated! But with each day that passed, I started feeling better and stronger. Until one day, it didn't hurt anymore. And the day I really let go was the day I met Terry, and I've never looked back. Terry loves and respects me unconditionally. I never would have known what true love was had I stayed in that abusive relationship with William. So, believe me when I say 'you will get through this!'"

We all hug Lela. She apologizes to me again and I accept. I tell everyone about my promotion and they're thrilled. Taylor walks towards the kitchen and brings out this beautifully wrapped box and hands it to me. "Natalie, we are all very proud of you, your courage, your drive. We wanted you to know how much we love you and we think you're well on your way to the top."

"What have you guys done?" I exclaim and I unwrap the box.

"Hurry up slow poke!" says Lela.

"Oh, this is so nice. I love it!" It's a burgundy leather-bound organizer.

"We figured you'd need this for all of your big time appointments after the television interview," says Renee.

"You guys are so sweet. I love you. The first thing I'll write in here is our meeting date for next month."

We pour ourselves another glass of wine, finish our food and talk until midnight. The consensus of the group is that I continue seeing Miles and that it would be no harm having lunch with Derrick. We're both adults and should be able to handle seeing each other. My mind agrees but my heart says that I have a surprise in store!

CHAPTER 22

Today was my first newscast as afternoon anchor at Channel 3. It was great! The weeks leading up to today were exhausting and exhilarating. I loved every moment of the preparation. Frank was not kidding when he said the staff would have me ready in no time. I feel so comfortable in the anchor seat. It is as if I have been anchoring all my life, it's the type of rush and completeness I can't describe. I'm nervous when I first sit down, but after I speak those first words, the butterflies disappear.

It's minutes after the newscast and Frank Holmes enters the studio. Brad and I glance at each other.

"Excellent job Natalie and Brad! Today's newscast was one of the best I've seen in a long time. You two work well together, great chemistry. I think we have a winner here."

"She's easy to work with, " Brad says while flashing his killer smile.

"Thanks Brad. You too. And thank you Frank, that means a lot coming from you."

"Oh, don't mention it. I just wanted to be the first to congratulate you two and say a job well done." He reaches toward us and shakes our hands.

"Brad?"

"Yes sir?"

"Are you getting use to this Vegas heat?

"Ah, it's not that bad. Coming from Texas, I can handle it."

"Well, good. You two continue the good work and I'll talk to you both later."

Neither of us can contain our smiles as Frank exits the studio. Suddenly, the room erupts. High fives are being slapped. Everyone yells. The entire crew is hype.

"See, we did it you guys. We did it!" yells our cameraman Gene.

"One down and hundreds to go!" Brad says.

"Well, I'm ready if you are Brad," I say.

"You betcha!"

"It was really nice working with you today Brad."

"Likewise Natalie. Let's call it a day!"

Brad Grisham is the new anchor from Dallas. He is extremely handsome for a white boy—no pun intended. He reminds me of a clean- cut Ridge Forrester off the soap opera *"The Bold & The Beautiful."* If I ever thought about sampling some vanilla pudding, it would be his type. Brad is very professional and has been completely helpful and patient during this preparation period. He's been married five years and has three kids. Never stops talking about his family and just lights up when he speaks of his children. It's beautiful to see. Brad has had a remarkable career path. He worked construction for several years as an electrician. How he got into broadcasting was a mere fluke. One day while working on a site in downtown Dallas, he witnessed a bank being robbed. The reporter covering the story was shot and unable to continue covering the robbery. Brad went to assist the reporter and wait for help to arrive. Right before the reporter blacked out, he handed Brad his mic. The cameraman was still shooting and turned to Brad for help. Brad turned toward the camera and started describing what he had witnessed. That evening Brad was the town hero and found a new niche. He says that it happened so fast that he never really had time to think about what he was doing. He's been smooth sailing ever since. It's amazing to me how both our careers took off through tragic situations.

We grab our scripts and head to the newsroom where everyone is cheering for the new mid-day duo. I'm on cloud nine. This is too good to be true and I'm lovin it! Everyone tells us how great the newscast was and leads us to a table where a huge cake in the shape of a television is waiting for us to cut.

Several minutes later, I walk to my desk and notice an envelope on my keyboard. I sit down and read the following: *Meet me at the Mirage at 7pm—-Room 2205. M*

I smile and immediately get butterflies. Our relationship has been wonderful. We've been hanging out with each other and spending quality time. Everyday we have lunch together and he's even gone to church with me several times. It's so nice, being able to really talk with someone and to have them show a genuine interest. Miles is so kind and such a gentleman. We've done lots of kissing and touching, but we haven't gone all the way.

There is no mistaking what tonight is about. We've been fighting it for a long time. Don't get me wrong, there have been some close calls, but we've always managed to cool off. Well so long cool …hello hot. Tonight is the night! I gotta run by Victoria's Secret.

CHAPTER 23

I arrive at the Mirage around 6:45 wearing a peach and cream slip dress with peach and cream snakeskin sandals and matching bag. My hair is up in a nice chignon.

Make-up very matte, very natural and soft. My one-piece strapless teddy from Victoria's Secret is definitely making things tighter and putting the cleavage right where it needs to be. I can tell it's in the right place by the looks I'm getting from men and women. Vegas is a trip.

I waste a little time by looking at the dolphins and white tigers on display. Just as I was entering the hotel the volcano erupted outside. The Mirage is breathtaking, not only is it beautiful outside, but the decor inside is incredible. Everyone has to visit this place at least once in their lifetime. At 7:10 I decide to go up to the room. My stomach is doing flips. I am so nervous. *Why are you so nervous Natalie? It's not like you've never had sex before!*

Yeah, but I've never had sex with Miles…dammit, I'm gonna faint! Okay Natalie, get a grip. I take a few breaths, step off the elevator and follow the signs to my room. There's a note on my door: *Come in and relax—-M*

The door is ajar. I walk in.

The room is breathtaking. Beautiful terracotta and cream marble floors with the most gorgeous Italian furniture I've ever laid eyes on. There are white rose petals scattered across the floor and bed. Approximately 20 white candles light the room. The curtains are open to a nicely decorated table on the balcony. I realize that I haven't moved since I stepped in the room. I sit my bag down and make myself comfortable. Just when I sit down there's a knock at the door.

"Who is it?"

"Room service."

"Room service? I didn't order room service." I open the door and four people are standing before me in starch white uniforms.

"Ms. Norwood?"

"Yes."

"We're here to set up dinner," they say while smiling as if they know something that I don't.

"Uh, okay. Help yourself."

I watch as these people turn the balcony into a formal dining room. This is too exciting! God I wish my girls could be flies on the wall. In less than 10 minutes everything is in place. One of the waiters walks back inside the room and turns the CD player on. Kenny G echoes through the room. I grab my purse to give them a tip.

"Excuse me miss, but that's already been taken care of."

"Well, thank you," I say

After they leave, I walk out onto the balcony and try to take in everything before me. I'm tempted to lift the lids off the food, but I don't. Whatever it is smells wonderful. I hear someone entering the room. I turn around. It's Miles. He's smiling. I walk back into the room.

"Hey, brown sugar!" he says as he lifts me off my feet into his arms.

"Hi Mil———." Before I can get his name out he's kissing me and taking my breath away slowly. He holds me tight. So tight I feel his heartbeat next to mine. He slides my body down his just slow enough where I can feel his nature rising.

"You hungry?" he asks

"Uhmmm, a little," I whisper. "Are you?"

"Yeah, I'm starving, " he says as he looks through me.

"Then by all means you should eat Miles."

"I thought you'd never ask," he says with a slight growl in his voice.

He walks toward the door and dims the lights. Only the flicker of the candles light the room. He walks toward me, takes off his shirt and unties his loosely fitted pants. They drop to the floor. Damn! I don't know how this is going to sound, but I have to say it: Miles has the biggest, most beautiful dick I have ever seen. It's perfect. The shape, the size, the color. Sounds a little pornographic, but if anyone was lucky enough to be where I'm standing, they'd say the same thing.

"I thought you wanted to eat?" I say shyly as he approaches me slowly.

"I do," he whispers in my ear. The heat of his breath sends chills through my body. He slips my dress off. I guess that's why they call it a slip dress.

"Natalie you are so beautiful," he says as he lets his fingertips brush against my nipples. "I've been thinking about you all day long. Kissing you, touching you. Damn, you're sexy."

He falls to his knees and starts exploring my body with his hands slowly, gently.

He pays attention to every curve, every detail.

"Thank you Family Fitness!" I say to myself, cuz the body is tight.

His touch is like a current through my body. Everywhere he touches is sensitive and hot. He's awakens parts of me with his hands that I thought were dead.

"Come here," he says in a tone that let's me know exactly what's on his mind. He lies on his back and reaches his hands to pull me toward him.

"Let me taste it," he moans as he positions me on his face. My world is completely cloudy now. No sense of direction or reality. Ecstasy consumes me. *This has to be a dream, because nothing on earth feels this good.* He lifts me onto the bed. My body yearns for him. I can't get enough of touching him, kissing him. He tastes good. He smells good. I want, I need to taste every inch of him. I am so hot. The intensity inside of me peaks. He grabs my breast and runs his tongue gently across the base. *Yes, I'm in fuckin heaven!*

"Oh, Miles!"

"Yes, baby."

"Mmmmm." I can't even get the words out,

"I know baby, I know." he says softly.

We kiss long and deep. I run my tongue across his teeth. I take his tongue and suck it slowly. He moans. I feel him teasing the doors of my paradise, just barely touching it. I reach for his passion. It's hard, rigid, pounding with desire. I know he aches for me because I feel the same power take over me. I arch towards him, signaling that I'm ready. He moans again and then stops. He opens the nightstand and pulls out some condoms. I grab one from him and slide it on gently. Slowly I let him enter. I close the doors on his love and take him on a ride he'll never forget. Our bodies are one. Our souls embrace.

There are no more words, only sounds of complete pleasure. We drown in an abyss of love. *Will we ever come up for air? I hope not.*

CHAPTER 24

Monday morning is here before I know it. This weekend just flew by. I'm still trying to come down from my high. Being with Miles was absolutely wonderful. No phone calls, no interruptions. Just an intense meeting of the body and mind. How we managed to find time to sleep and eat is amazing to me. We could not get enough of each other. Waking up those few days in his arms was complete heaven. I can't really describe it, other than it was perfect, like I was meant to be in his arms forever. It was too right, if there's such a thing. It's kind of scary for me having feelings like this for someone again, but it seems different with Miles. He's so easy to be with.

After greeting a few people in the newsroom, I head to my desk and notice a huge vase of lavender tulips. My heart is fluttering because I know that they are from Miles. I quickly grab the card and tear it open.

I want you, I miss you, I need you in my life.

Derrick

P.S. Please call me at 396-0101

Oh my god, Derrick. I completely forgot about him. What am I going to do with these flowers? I can't let Miles see these. Shoot, here he comes.

"Nice flowers," he says with a slight edge to his voice.

"Yeah, they're ok," I say trying to sound unimpressed.

"Someone's beggin' and doing a good job I might add!" I can see the anger across his face.

"Miles, it's not what you think."

"And how do you know what I'm thinking? Are you psychic now?" he snaps.

"Well, you sound pretty irritated, " I respond while trying to keep my voice calm and not draw attention to us.

"Wouldn't you be irritated if you spent the weekend with a wonderful man and you come to work and find flowers on his desk from another woman? Come on Nat, don't play me!"

"Miles, I am not playing you. How was I to know that someone would be sending me flowers? You act like I planned this." Now I'm getting pissed. "And you didn't know who could be sending me flowers. For all you know it could be anybody. My sister or my father. You immediately jump to the conclusion that they're from a man."

"Are you trying to say that their not?"

"I'm not saying anything. You haven't given me a chance to say anything. You were pissed off before I got here and had already come to your own conclusion."

"Whatever Natalie."

"Whatever. Is that all you have to say?" I ask slightly shocked at his reaction. Miles turns to walk away and nearly bumps into, guess who? *Derrick! Fuck! Fuck! Fuck! I am going to shit on myself right now. What the hell is happening? I was just in fucking paradise having multiple orgasms. Damn, ain't life grand!*

"Hi beautiful! Am I interrupting something?" Derrick asks as he walks towards me and gives me a lingering kiss just close enough to my mouth to make my body react. *I hate him.*

"Derrick, what are you doing here?" I ask in total disbelief.

"Well, you wouldn't return a brotha's call, so I decided to drop by." Miles observes everything very closely. His temples pulse.

"Uh, Miles, this is Derrick. Derrick this is Miles." I stammer through the introductions. They greet each other and shake hands. I turn to Miles. "Miles, can we talk later?"

"Sure Nat, later." The look on Miles' face says it all. I know that he's hurt and I know what he's thinking, but there's nothing I can do right now. Derrick is standing here with this grin on his face. "Brotha don't look too happy." he says.

"Shut up Derrick. What are you doing here?" I ask angrily.

"I told you that I needed to talk to you."

"And I told you that I didn't have anything to say to you."

"Natalie, please. Give me a few minutes. Hear me out. Please babylove." *Oh, why did he have to call me that? I used to melt every time I heard those words.*

"Derrick, I have to prepare for my newscast."

"Tonight, meet me for dinner at Ruth's Chris Steakhouse at 7," he pleads as he grabs my hands.

"I'll think about it," I snap.

"I'll be waiting," he says as he leans towards me again and kisses me on my neck. "I never stopped loving you." He walks away. The smell of L'eau D'issey lingers in the air. I'd know his scent anywhere. I feel a tingle in my stomach. *Help me Jesus, cuz I'm about to go crazy. What am I going to do? Derrick Foster, the love of my life. I slept with this man's sweater for two years at Grambling. I loved his body, his style, his charisma, his laugh, his walk, his voice, his mind, his touch, his kiss. Damn! I just loved him. No man has ever captured my heart the way he did. It's taken years to get over him and now here he comes again. Men ain't shit! When you're suckin' their dick they don't know how to treat you and as soon as they think you're suckin' someone else's dick, they pop up talking about lovin' you. And as mad as I am, images and memories of suckin' Derrick's dick are popping up in my mind. Damn, that was some good dick.*

I have to laugh at the thought because right now my mind is discombobulated. I need to talk to my sister. She'll tell me what to do.

I dial her number and while I'm waiting for her to pick up I scope the newsroom to see if Miles is in sight. He's nowhere to be found. Shoot!

"Hello."

"Hi sister dear."

"Hey, what's up?"

"Day, you'll never guess what just happened!"

"What? You sound really messed up."

"Derrick showed up at my job."

"Girl, shut up!" Day says with a laugh.

"I'm serious Day, and he sent flowers before he came, and Miles saw the flowers, and I had to introduce them and girl the shit just hit the fan!"

"Oooooh, what are you going to do?"

"Day, why do you think I'm calling you?"

"Okay, calm down Natalie. Where is Derrick?"

"He's gone. He wants me to meet him for dinner, but I don't know."

"What do you mean you don't know? Go! You are not married to either of them. They are both your friends. I don't see any harm in going to dinner with Derrick."

"But Day, what about Miles? I really care about him."

"And?" she asks dumbfoundedly.

"And it hurt his feelings seeing flowers from another man after we had such a wonderful weekend." I plead with Day to try and understand.

"And what does that have to do with anything? You two just started seeing each other. Listen here little sister, don't put all of your eggs in one basket. You are a single, educated, not to mention fine like your sister, attractive, black woman with options. Enjoy both of them. Men do it all the time. Why can't we? Shoot, I'd go to dinner and see what's up with Derrick. There may be some flames waiting to be rekindled, and Miles will get over it. It's not like you two are in love."

"But Day, I really care about Miles. He is so sweet and I think we could be good for each other."

"Do you still have feelings for Derrick?"

"It's been a long time."

"That's not what I asked you. Do you still care for Derrick?"

"Day, I don't know!"

"Yes you do. That's why you're so hesitant to go out with him. You've never gotten over him. Miss Organized is unorganized." She laughs uncontrollably."

"Sister dear, I'm serious. This is not funny." I'm slightly angry.

"Okay. Are you and Miles an official couple?"

"We're close." I say.

"That's not what I asked you."

"Day, we haven't said that we're going together, but we spend all of our time together and this weekend was very special."

"If it has not been verbalized, you are still single and free. Miles will just have to swallow his pride. Go on and have dinner with Derrick. Who knows what might happen?"

"That just sounds so cold and I really care for Miles."

"Yeah, but you really loved Derrick. What's wrong with hearing him out?"

"That's just it Day. When he's near me I still get these feelings and it scares me."

"Why? You're human."

"I know. I just don't want to go through the same crap again."

"You guys were babies Nat. Now you're both older and more mature. Who knows what's in store? Shit, be daring!"

"Thanks Day. You've really made this easy for me." I say sarcastically.

"Hey, I try!"

"I'll call you later."

"I love you Nat! Bye."

"Bye, Day."

Now I'm more confused than before. What the hell am I going to do? Maybe I will go to dinner with Derrick. What could it hurt? Anyhow, Miles is mad as hell and I need to let him calm down. I open the letter on my desk. It's from Antonio.

Dear Natalie,

What's up? Nothing much here. I mean how much can I do in camp? I have been making the most of my time though. I took your advice and I'm taking my GED in three weeks. After that, I'll start studying for the ACT and SAT. I can't believe how much I like math and English. This stuff is tight once you understand it. I always thought school was so hard, but it's not. One of the inmates has been tutoring me since I got up in here and I'm just taking it all in. I can't wait to get out. Thanks to you and Miles testifying, I'll have another chance. This time I won't mess up. Good looking outs for the care package. My mom came by to see me last week. She looks really good. The re-hab is helping a lot. Thanks again for really being a friend, tell Miles I said what's up.

Antonio

I always get misty when I get letters from Antonio. He has made such a turn-a-round. I remember that day in court as if it were yesterday. Antonio looked helpless in that official orange prison uniform. His hands and feet were shackled. A few of his relatives showed up in court along with his mom. Antonio's mom was frail. The effects of crack cocaine were quite evident. However, she was clean. The hearing was several hours long and it was very painful re-living that horrible night. Based on Miles and my testimonies, the judge showed leniency and sentenced

Antonio to the Nevada Boot and Education Youth Camp for teens who commit violent crimes. The judge felt that the circumstances surrounding Antonio's childhood were so devastating that he was literally thrown into a life of crime. The boot camp is highly favored and one could only get in and by-pass the prison system through a judges recommendation. Once accepted into the camp, Antonio has to complete high school and take college or trade courses. He also has to work a part-time job at the camp where his wages are put into a savings account until he is released.

Plus, he has to volunteer his time once a week at a local elementary school where he talks to kids about the dangers of joining a gang and selling drugs.

By far, this is the best thing that could happen to Antonio. I cannot imagine what life would have been for him in prison. I think I'll go see him next week. Maybe Miles will go with me. That is if he's speaking to me. He hasn't been back to my desk since Derrick left. I better let things cool off and call him later.

CHAPTER 25

I cannot believe that I am pulling into the parking lot of Ruth's Chris Steak House. Have I lost my mind? I should have called an emergency sisterfriends meeting to discuss this whole Derrick issue again. But no, my fast ass is meeting him for dinner. Why couldn't I just say no? I mean I just had a fantastic weekend with Miles and things are really going well between us. He is so sweet and romantic and here I am meeting Derrick. Okay, it's only dinner, I better keep telling myself that. I pull out my compact and touch up my make-up before getting out of the car. I feel the butterflies twirling in my stomach. I take a deep breath and head towards the door. "Natalie, it's only dinner!" I say aloud. Collecting my composure, I step through the door.

"Ms. Norwood?" A maitre d' in a black tuxedo, crisp white shirt and goatee waits for me. "This way please."

I follow him into the private dining room, which is elegantly decorated in cream and gold. Candles illuminate the room. Derrick is looking out of a window and turns when he hears us enter. He looks wonderful in his navy, three-piece Hugo Boss suit. A navy and yellow jacquard tie and handkerchief accent the suit perfectly. Nothing about him has changed.

"Ah, you found her," Derrick says while walking towards me with his heart-melting smile.

"Well Mr. Foster," says the maitre d', "you did say that I would recognize her immediately."

Derrick interjects, "Yeah, she's not easy to miss. Thanks Pierre."

"My pleasure sir." He turns towards me and bows slightly. "Ms Norwood."

"Thank you," I say.

Derrick takes my hands and pulls me towards him. My body immediately responds. He just holds me close to him without saying a word. I start to remember how good it feels to be in his arms. I try to pull away. He gently grabs my face and kisses me softly.

"Thank you for coming Natalie. I've missed you."

"Really?" I say nonchalantly.

"Yes I have."

"If you say so."

He pulls my chair out and I sit down. I notice everything is perfect. Totally Derrick. His charm and sense of style permeates the room. Derrick sits down and leans on the dining table.

"Where do I begin?" he asks.

"The beginning is always good," I say trying not to sound too snappy.

"Well," he takes a deep breath and looks me intensely in the eyes, "I have so much that I need to say to you. Things that I should have said a long time ago, but was too immature to say so."

"Derrick, maybe some things are better off not said," I say.

"No Natalie." He reaches for my hand. "Some things need to be said."

He kisses the palms of my hands and I pull away. Small currents rush through my body.

"But like you've said, you can't fix all the pain you've caused in my life."

"This is true Nat, but I believe that I can bring happiness into your life." *Is he being sincere? Can I trust Derrick again?*

I lean slightly over the table and say, "Derrick, do you not think that I can be happy without you? What the hell do you think I've been since we broke up? Fucking miserable? Well, I'm sorry to ruin your poor, distressed image of me. I have been wonderful."

"Natalie, babylove, calm down. Why are you so defensive? I didn't say that. I just meant that I want to make you happier baby. Please baby, let me make you happier."

He gets up from his chair and walks over to me. Derrick pulls me up towards him and holds me gently. He caresses my back softly. He lifts my chin and kisses me. My lips part and I feel his tongue explore my mouth. My body reacts.

"I want you Natalie," he whispers.

"Why Derrick?" I pause to get my composure. "Why me? After all this time?" I ask.

"Because you were the best thing that ever happened in my life and I fucked up, but not again. This time it's going to be right."

"This time?" Looking at him with questionable eyes. "What makes you think that I want you back in my life?" I ask.

"Listen, let's just enjoy our dinner and we'll see where it leads us. Okay, babylove?" He's still holding me in his arms.

I caught that 'where it leads us' crap. I am not going to let Derrick disrupt my world. Natalie, enjoy your free meal and take your behind home.

"Sure, let's enjoy our meal," I say.

"Good. That's what I wanted to hear," he says with a smile.

CHAPTER 26

Why I agreed to have a nightcap with Derrick is beyond me, but here I am in his lush condo overlooking the entire city. Vegas is so beautiful at night. Growing up here I never paid serious attention to this mecca, but moments like this really make me appreciate my hometown.

Derrick's condo is just how I pictured it would be. Completely laid. It's tastefully done in wonderful earth tones, accented with rich, warm browns, burnt orange and olive. Nothing is out of place. African sculptures adorn mantel. Paintings by Albert Fennel and Charles Bibbs hang throughout the room. A stack of pine grid chests are open slightly with cable chenille throws peeking from each. Burgundy, gold, royal blue and brown pillows are scattered everywhere.. A large, oversized chocolate sofa sits in the middle of the room. One cannot help but be comfortable in this room. It instantly makes me want to lay down. *I wonder why?* I sit on the sofa. I feel as if I'm sitting on clouds.

"Make yourself at home," Derrick yells from the kitchen. "I'll be out in a sec."

"I'm not staying long," I say sarcastically. Derrick walks out of the kitchen carrying a wooden platter with an assortment of cheeses, crackers, fruit and a bottle of wine. As he walks towards me I notice that he's taken off his jacket and tie. His shirt is unbuttoned revealing the fine hairs on his chest and tight stomach. *His body is still cut. Damn.*

"Here babylove," he says as he hands me a glass of wine.

"Thank you."

He eases next to me on the couch so that there is no room between us. "What shall we toast to Nat?" he asks suggestively.

"I don't know, you tell me."

"How about to new beginnings?"

"Sure."

We lift our glasses. Derrick leans back and stares at me intensely.

"What's wrong Derrick?"

"Nothing. Absolutely nothing," he says with a slight smile.

I sit my glass on the table. "Derrick I th…."

He places his fingers on my lips.

"Shhh baby," he says softly while moving even closer to me. "Come here, sit between my legs." He sits our glasses on the coffee table, gently pulls me between his legs and starts massaging my scalp. He knows that I love to have my scalp massaged. It's so relaxing. *I should get my butt up right now, but noooooo I'm sitting my little ass right here.*

"You used to love for me to do this. Does it feel good baby?"

"Yes," I whisper, barely audible.

"I love your hair. It's so soft and it always smells good. Mmmm." He leans towards me and kisses my ear. "You smell good," he whispers in my ear.

I feel myself leaving earth. He has always been able to just touch me and I melt. I turn towards him. "Derrick listen." I try to plea, but he kisses me like we've been kissing all of our life. No test kiss. No getting use to each other all over again . No, this man kisses me like I like to be kissed. He takes my tongue softly and sucks it gently. He runs his tongue across my teeth. He tenderly licks my lips. I feel his hands explore my body. He knows where to touch. I feel my clothes being removed and I instinctively start to take his off. I can't control myself. It's like this huge void in my body, mind and soul is filling up, and it feels so good.

We're both naked and he pulls me on top of him and starts caressing my body softly, slowly.

He pulls my hair back from my face. "Natalie, I love you with all my heart and I want you back."

"Derrick, how do you know that I am truly what you want? And how do I know that you are not going to rip my heart to pieces again?" Tears stream down my face. So much has built up inside of me.

"Babylove, I promise you that I'll never hurt you again. No matter how many relationships I've had, I can't get you out of my head. Something has always been missing in my life, and that something is you."

We sit up. He wipes my eyes. "I hurt you Natalie and that's something that I'll always regret, but I can't live my life without you. I am half of a man without you and I need you to make me whole. Please come back to me." He's on his knees and we're both crying.

"Derrick, I just don't know. So much has happened. Time has passed. Things are different."

"That's true Nat, but that doesn't mean that we can't start over. Come here," he says pulling me on the floor with him. "We'll take it one day at a time."

"Okay. One day at a time," I say.

"Now come here and let Daddy make it purr." We both laugh. He lifts me off the rug and takes me into his bedroom. He lays me on my stomach and kneels between my legs. Slowly he pours some vanilla oil in his palms and rubs his hands together until the oil is slightly warm. He massages my butt with a certain firmness. Softly he kisses my burning cheeks and makes sure both are satisfied. Then he runs his tongue up my spine. I shiver in delight. His hands are everywhere and my body responds passionately to his touch. I turn over and grab him by his neck and pull him on top of me. I kiss him deeply. "Let me taste it baby," Derrick whispers. He slides down and treats my kitty like a full course meal. *Oh, the kitty is purring now!* Just when I'm about to come he inserts a finger and brings me to greater heights.

"Ooh baby, that feels so good," I moan.

"I know baby, I know," he says. My body tingles. I reach for his hardened rod and stroke him gently. I tease the tip with my tongue. He moans. I lick his inner thighs before taking him deeply into my mouth. His back arches arches and his hips slowly rotate as I give him the blow of a lifetime. He climbs the walls. *Shoot, I'm impressing myself. Maybe I just want him to remember what he left.*

"Can I have some?" Derrick pants.

"All you want baby," I say.

He reaches in his nightstand and puts on a condom. Entering my paradise slowly he says, "Damn, it's still tight. Shit this feels good."

"You like it tight, don't you?" I ask.

"Yes babylove."

"I know baby. Mmmm work it. That's it. That's the spot baby."

Uncontrollable passion and two condoms later, we're exhausted.

SEASONS CHANGE

CHAPTER 27

A few months have passed since Derrick and I have started seeing each other again. It's been wonderful. However, it's hell trying to juggle my life between Derrick and Miles. I can't seem to decide who I want to be with. To be perfectly honest, I really don't want to choose. All of my needs are being met by both of these men. I know that it's selfish on my part to want them both and I know that eventually I'll have to choose, but for now I'm just going to enjoy this bliss.

It's raining outside and I decide to open all of my windows and let the breeze in. As I place my teakettle on the stove, the telephone rings.

"Hello."

"Hey Nat, it's Miles."

"Hi honey. How are you?"

"Um, I'm ok." There's tension in his voice.

"You don't sound ok. What's wrong?"

"Can I stop by? We need to talk." *This sounds serious.*

"Sure babe, come on."

"I'll be there shortly."

"Ok."

We hang up. I wonder what's wrong with Miles. Maybe he's upset that I didn't call last night. Derrick and I had dinner and I didn't get in until late. Well, whatever it is, he's on his way so I'd better freshen up.

I shower and put on some denim cut-offs and a white cotton shirt. I pin my hair up and powder my face. No makeup, just a little gloss on my lips. Casual, but cute. I open the door to let Pooch out and Miles is standing at the door. He looks good in his navy Nautica shirt and shorts.

"Hey handsome," I say, as I reach towards him to give him a kiss and hug.

"Hey." He responds dryly and lightly pushes me away as he walks into my apartment.

"Well, hello to you too. What's wrong with you?" I ask as I close the door behind him. He turns around and just stares at me. His eyes are cold. His face is sad.

"Miles, honey, talk to me." I caress his arm. He walks away and sits on the couch. I sit next to him silently waiting for him to say something. I notice a tear running down his cheek.

"Baby, what's wrong? I can't help you if you don't talk to me," I say.

He faces me and speaks slowly and softly, "Natalie, I love you. I mean I really love you."

"I love y...."

"Stop!" He holds up his hand. "Don't say it Nat. Don't say that you love me."

"But I do love you Miles." I say as I reach for his hand. He backs away from me and stands up. "Then why the fuck were you out with Derrick last night?"

I'm stunned.

"Answer me Nat! Why the fuck do I go into a restaurant last night and see you all hugged up with this brotha if you love me?"

Miles is steaming and justly so. I know that he's hurting.

"Miles," I say very softly. "I'm sorry."

"What are you sorry about Nat? Sorry that you were in my arms the night before? Sorry that you weren't secretive enough? Damn, I must be a fuckin' fool. Something told me that this Derrick guy was more than just an ex showing up. And you assured me that it was over. Why Nat? Why couldn't you just be honest?" Miles angrily paces the floor.

"Miles, I wanted to be honest, but I was confused. I mean I am confused. I have never been in a situation like this before where my feelings are torn between two people. I do love you Miles, but there's a part of me that hasn't ever stop loving Derrick." Tears start to flow from my eyes. I feel Miles' pain.

"Natalie, I cannot share you. I won't share you. You obviously have some unfinished business with this guy." He walks towards me. His voice falters. "When I'm with you, I'm yours body, heart and soul." Miles places my arms around his waist and holds me closely, "When I'm in these arms, I am filled. You are my world, but I want you to be happy. If this brotha' makes you happy, then I'll back out."

"But Miles!" I plead.

"Shhhh, baby," he whispers in my ear. "I want you to know that I don't think any less of you, because I know that you're a good woman and you would never purposely hurt anyone. But you need to be honest with yourself sweetheart. If you love this man, don't half step." Miles lifts my chin and kisses me softly. He kisses me as if he's taking in every inch of me. My crying worsens. "Don't cry baby," he says.

"But Miles, you just don't understand," I say.

"Listen Nat, more than anything in this world I want you to be happy. Yeah, I want to be the one bringing a smile to this beautiful face, but if I can't be the one, I have to accept it."

He wipes my face with his shirt and I reach up and wipe his tears away. "I love you Natalie Norwood." He smiles slightly and walks out the door.

"Miles, Miles!" I scream his name, but he doesn't return.

Oh God, please tell me that this is not happening. I feel as if my best friend has just walked out of my life. How could I let this happen? Miles, I do love you. I do. I cry long and hard.

My heart aches. I've known for months that eventually I'd have to choose between Miles and Derrick, but I never imagined the pain. What were you thinking Natalie? There could be no happy ending, someone was going to get hurt. Oh, Miles I am so sorry. I'm numb. What am I going to do now? I've just lost this wonderful, loving man. What if it doesn't work between Derrick and I? What if Miles was the one? Dammit Natalie! All of these images of Miles and I flash through my mind. I miss him already. Maybe, I'll call him. But what do I say? This is a mess. I need some air. I hear Pooch scratching at the door. I let her in and quickly change into my workout gear. The gym, that's exactly what I need.

CHAPTER 28

"And that's it for our afternoon report. I'm Natalie Norwood."

"And I'm Brad Grisham. See you back here at five. Thanks for joining us."

"That's a wrap guys. Good show," yells Tony our cameraman.

I gather my scripts and get up from my chair. "Hey Natalie, I don't mean to impose and if I'm out of order let me know."

"Sure Brad, what's up?"

With this very concerned look he asks, "Natalie, what's going on with you?"

"What do you mean Brad?" I say coyly, not really wanting to give up information.

"I mean, what's bothering you?" he asks.

"Nothing," I say matter of factly.

"Oh, come on Natalie. Everyone has noticed how quiet and withdrawn you've become. Sure, on the air you're poised and professional, but as soon as those cameras go off, you go into a shell. Is it Miles?"

I'm slightly shocked. "Why would you think that?"

Brad pushes away from the news desk. "Listen, if you don't want to talk about this just say so and I'll understand. But I know that something is bothering you."

He stands and starts to walk away.

"Okay Brad. But promise me. This stays between us."

"Promise."

I explain the entire situation to Brad and he listens intently with a keen reporter's ear. I can see his investigative mind at work. Then out of the blue he starts laughing. "Brad, this is not funny. I'm serious," I say sternly.

"I'm sorry Natalie, but get real." He leans forward. "Let me get this straight. You're dating Miles and the ex–boyfriend shows up. You start dating your ex and Miles finds out. Miles ends the relationship." He pauses. "And you're upset? Come on sweetie. How long did you think you could have your cake and eat it too?"

I'm too surprised at his bluntness. "Brad!"

"Natalie, I hate to burst your bubble, but I'm with Miles. Either be with this Derrick guy or cut ties with him and be with Miles. You can't expect for Miles to just hang around. Come on, you wouldn't do it. Think about it."

"I know, I know, but I love them both," I say, trying to get Brad on my side.

"That may be true, but you can't have them both."

"Shit! Men do it all the time," I snap.

"Don't kid yourself doll. I'm a man and I've done some messed up shit before. Yeah, I've had two women before and believe me, it was not worth it. I almost lost my wife because of my dick." He laughs. "Excuse my French. If had to do it all over again, I never would have made those mistakes. Don't confuse great sex with love. Too many smart women do. I'm not saying that you shouldn't be sexually fulfilled, but look for someone that can make love to your mind as well. Now, all you have to decide is which one is just a lover and which one is your soul mate. Being torn between two lovers is no joke."

This white boy is really breaking things down. I can't believe it.

"So, do I really just let Miles go?"

"For now, yes. Obviously you feel the need to give this Derrick guy a second chance. Go on and see it through, so you never have that 'what if' question in your mind. If it works great, and if not, at least you'll know."

"It just hurts so much and I never meant to hurt Miles. He is such a wonderful man." I say trying not to get teary.

"Yeah, Miles is a good guy, but he deserves you completely," Brad says as he pats my shoulder. "You'll be ok and I'm here as a friend if you ever need me."

"Thanks Brad."

"Anytime." Brad walks out of studio leaving me with an awful lot to ponder.

CHAPTER 29

The newsroom is in a frenzy as usual. There has been a robbery at First American Bank downtown. Rhonda is covering the story live. I walk over to my desk and check my voice mail. Naomi, Renee and Taylor call me on three-way to remind me of our meeting coming up and also to see if I had spoken with Lela. Day called and chewed me out for not touching base all week. And my last message is from Derrick. "Hey babylove, it's me Derrick. I can't make dinner tonight. I have an important engagement and probably won't get in until late. I'll call you tomorrow. I love you."

Mmmm, Derrick is canceling dinner. I wonder what that's about? Whatever. I need to get away. Let me call Day and tell her that I'm coming to Virginia for the weekend. Just as I'm about to make the call to Day I hear voices near me, and one of the voices is Miles. I turn and see Miles talking to an attractive sister. She's about 5'8, dark complexion and closely cropped hair. They're both laughing and being quite touchy. It's apparent that there's something going on there. Miles leans towards this woman and gives her a light peck on the lips. She giggles and walks out of the newsroom. Miles turns to walk into the studio and our eyes meet. He has this look in his eyes that question whether or not I just witnessed what happened. He slowly approaches my desk.

"Hi Natalie," he says softly.

"Hello Miles."

"So," he pauses, "How are you?"

"I'm good Miles. And yourself?" I ask.

"I'm living," he says with a slight smile.

"I can see that!" I say with a slight edge.

"And exactly what do you mean by that?" he asks while closing the gap between us.

"I just mean that I can see that you have gone on with your life," I say nonchalantly.

"Was I not supposed to?" he asks with this look of puzzlement.

"I didn't say that Miles."

"Well, there was definitely some implication in your statement." He narrows his eyes and shows a bit of anger.

"Whatever Miles!" I snap.

"No, it's not whatever Natalie. Let's step outside." He takes my arm firmly without drawing any attention and we walk outside. Miles looks around to make sure that we're alone.

"What's your problem Natalie?"

"I don't have a problem," I say while shifting my weight and crossing my arms.

He shakes his head in disbelief and thinks carefully about what his next words will be.

"Yeah Natalie, you have a problem and I'm gonna tell you what it is." I look away as if I'm not interested in what he's about to say.

"Look at me Nat." He grips my chin and turns my face towards him.

"You wanted your cake and to eat it too. You got caught. You had to make a choice. You chose Derrick. I bowed out gracefully. I go on with my life. Today you see me with someone else and you're pissed. Why?" He pauses for a moment. He gets no response from me.

"Why Natalie? I didn't cheat on you. I didn't choose another woman over you. You made this bed. Now you lie the fuck in it!"

I am in total shock that he is talking this way to me. I don't say a word.

"The bottom line is this: Either you want me or you don't. If you do, tell me right now and everyone in my life becomes ghost, but if not, don't hate me for going on without you. I love you Natalie Norwood, but a brotha just can't be your fool." There are tears in his eyes. He holds my face gently and with both hands kisses my forehead.

"Later," he whispers.

I stand there in a daze. *Did this man just actually tell me off? I cannot believe this shit, but then again, I can. I hurt him and everything he said was correct whether I want to admit it or not. Yes, I messed up this time. I do miss him. Now, what am I going to do?*

CHAPTER 30

I arrive in Virginia just around midnight. Day was insistent that she and Bryson pick me up from National, but I told her that the drive would do me good. As I drive to Woodbridge I start to really question my decision. Did I do the right thing in choosing Derrick or am I trying to recapture the past? Miles is an exceptional man. Romantic, kind, funny. The list goes on and on. Yet, I gave him up. *God you are really going to have to help me on this one. Please give me a sign as to whether or not I made the right choice.*

Virginia is beautiful even at night. The trees. The land. It's always so refreshing for me to visit. I love the desert with all of its mountainous surroundings, but I long for this type of greenery every now and then. My sister lives in this plush upper-middle class neighborhood. All the homes sit on an acre or more. Each home has its own distinct look. Day and Bryson chose a three-level brick colonial design. As I pull up to the house, I notice my sister is sitting out on the porch. She gets up and walks towards the car.

"Hi sister dear!" she exclaims.

"Hi sister." We embrace. Day looks good. She's wearing gray sweatpants and an olive colored sweatshirt. Her curly hair is cut extremely short and tapered very neatly. Day doesn't wear makeup. Her skin is flawless. People always laugh when they meet her because she's so tiny. Maybe 95 pounds on a good day, but she is full of fire.

"I'm so glad you came Nat. I've missed my sister," we're smiling.

"Me too. Why are you sitting out here?" I ask.

"Well, the boys are sleep and Bryson is working on a proposal for his job, so I just decided to wait out here for you. Plus, we can sit out here and talk for a while." Day puts her arm in mine and we walk to the porch and sit on the swing.

"I made us some tea." Day reaches for a thermos and pours us both a cup of herb tea. She has lemon and honey sitting on a small wicker table.

"Thanks Day."

"Okay, so tell me what's going on with you. How are you and Derrick doing?"

"Derrick and I are okay. He's been busy with lots of meetings lately."

"Is it what you expected? I mean the whole return to love thing?" Day is so point blank.

"Day things are great with Derrick. I love being with him, but I can't seem to shake Miles. As much as I've tried that man stays on my mind. And even though my relationship with Derrick is going well, I uhh."

"You what?"

"I don't know."

"Natalie, please do not say that you don't know. We always know. Now what is it?"

"Day, I've just been having a feeling about Derrick. I can't put my finger on it, but something isn't right. It's like this whole thing with him is too good to be true. I mean really. Like just before I left Vegas he left me a message canceling our dinner plans. He said that he had an important business meeting."

"And?" Day asks.

"Day he has had these late business meetings six times in the last two weeks. Now how many business meetings last after midnight?" I ask.

"Well, have you discussed it with him?"

"No, not yet."

"That's what you need to do. Don't walk around with this shit all built up inside of you and never, I mean never, disregard your instinct. Okay? Remember what I've taught you." She pats my hand and smiles.

"Yeah." I reply.

"And what's up with the sisterfriends?"

"Oh, everyone is fine except for Lela. She hasn't spoken to any of us in a while."

"Why?"

"We don't know. She just freaked out when I told everyone that I was considering giving Derrick another chance. I mean she flipped sister. Isn't that strange?" I ask while thinking about what I just said.

"Listen, I told you a long time ago that Lela was jealous of you. She has been every since high school. I know that you guys are best friends, but I never really felt like she was a true friend. She is just so sneaky to me."

"Day, don't say that about Lela. She's just going through something right now."

"Okay, she's going through something. You just keep your eyes and ears open little sis."

"I hear you," I sigh.

We finish our tea and get my things out of the car. As we enter the house, I can hear Bryson still pounding away at his computer.

"Hey brother dear!" I yell.

"Hey sis. How was your flight?" Bryson spins around in his chair. He's a handsome man. The color of brown leather. Tall, slender build. Kinda conservative. He's wearing a pair of Docker's and a tee shirt.

"It was nice."

"Glad you're here." He walks towards me and gives me a hug.

"Me too." I say.

"Well, I know that you and your sister will be talking all night so I'll talk to you later."

"Honey!" Day says.

"Honey nothing. You and Nat will be up all night. You forget, I know you." We all laugh.

Day and I go into the guest bedroom and finish our talk. We finally begin to tire out around 3am. After I shower and change into my pajamas, I lie in bed a few minutes and ponder over the Lela situation. Why would Lela just blow up? Why is she not speaking to me? *Could it be that Lela? Nahh, don't even go there Natalie.* I say my prayers and fall into a deep sleep.

CHAPTER 31

My weekend at Day's was great. We all went rollerblading. I fell about 10 times before I got the hang of it. Gabe and Galen are getting so big. Of course we went shopping at Potomic Mills Mall. I love that place. I feel rejuvenated.

We've decided to meet at my place for our sisterfriends session. To my knowledge, no one has heard from Lela. I left two messages on her machine today about tonight's meeting. This whole situation is so strange. I have never gone more than a few days without speaking to Lela. We have been friends since the fourth grade. As a matter of fact, Lela, Taylor and myself all attended the same elementary, junior high and high schools. We were known as The Three Musketeers, because when you saw one, you knew that the other two were not far behind. It was no surprise that we all decided to attend Grambling State University together. A week before we were scheduled to leave, Taylor's parents had some financial problems and she had to stay in Vegas and attend UNLV. Lela and I left for Grambling. I can't imagine my life without her. We've done everything together. I mean everything. We got our periods in the same month. We had our first sexual experience with twin brothers. We smoked our first joint together. Now that was funny. We just couldn't get the inhaling part straight, sorta like President Clinton. Anyway, I hope that whatever is bothering Lela will be over soon. I miss her.

Everyone arrives on time. That's the one thing we have stuck to from the beginning, that we would start all of our sessions on time. To no one's surprise, Lela doesn't show.

"I am sick of this shit! Let's just drive over to her house and see what's bothering her!" shouts Renee.

"I agree with Renee. This whole avoidance thing is getting on my last nerve," says Naomi.

"Whatever is going on, we need to find out and be through with it. If Lela doesn't want to be a part of our group any longer she needs to let us know, so we can stop worrying about her." Taylor adds.

"I'm there with all of you. Something is definitely going on and we need to find out tonight," I say.

"You know what bugs me out about this whole thing?" Renee asks.

"What?" asks Taylor.

"This whole thing started that night when we were talking about Derrick. So, what's with that?" Renee says.

"I don't know, but it's weird." Naomi interjects.

"Natalie, have you talked to Derrick about this?" Taylor asks.

"No, I was going to talk to him tonight. We had planned an early dinner before this meeting, but he called and cancelled saying that he had a business meeting." I say.

"Well, let's just drive over to her place and see what's up." Naomi says.

"That's right. Let's get this over with tonight," I say.

Renee asks if we should call first. "No!" says Taylor. "You know that she's screening her calls. Let's just go."

We all agree and head out of the door. Naomi decides to drive. For some reason the statement that Day made in Virginia about Lela being sneaky creeps into my mind. Butterflies invade the core of my stomach. I feel something dreadful, almost uncanny approaching. This is scary because my gut feeling has never failed me.

CHAPTER 32

It takes about 15 minutes to get to the Tropicana Villa Estates. The Estates are plush, Mediterranean style condos that start at $200,000. Lela's grandparents bought it for her twenty-fifth birthday. Some birthday present, huh? Lela's family is well off, but she has always been very down-to-earth. When we arrive, there is a car in front of us pulling into the security gate and so we just drive through. As we're pulling in front of Lela's condo, I notice a black Benz parked in front. Not just any Benz, but Derrick's. There is only one custom made Benz in Las Vegas with "SUCCESS" on the license plates. I can feel my heart picking up speed. Before I could say anything Taylor says it.

"Oh shit! Isn't that Derrick's car?"

"Natalie, let's just turn around. I don't want to see this shit," says Naomi.

"No!" I exclaim. "We are going to find out why my man's car is at my best friends house when his ass is supposed to be at a business meeting!"

I couldn't get out of the car fast enough. I step onto the sidewalk and freeze. Renee takes hold of my arm.

"Nat, we do not have to do this," she whispers. "Yes, Renee we do," I say.

We all walk slowly towards the door. As we approach the door, we hear jazz playing. I take a deep breath and knock on the door. The door isn't closed completely. It swings open.

God, I feel ill. My stomach is in knots. I'm having a hard time breathing. Someone grabs my hand. I push the door open wider. The scent of jasmin permeates the air. Candles are lit everywhere. Quite the romantic ambiance. We're all very tense. As we each step into the foyer all of our eyes immediately focus on the trail of clothes leading to the bedroom area. I gasp.

"Are you okay?" Naomi asks.

"I'm okay," I say, but I'm not.

I take a few steps and lean down and pick up a sweater. It's Derrick's. I put it up to my face. It's his scent. I hold the sweater close to my heart and proceed to walk down the hallway. In this moment I realize that my life is about to change. I already know, but I have to see it. I have to see it with my own eyes. God, this just can't be happening. Before we get to the bedroom, we hear it. Sounds of passion. Moans of pleasure. Words I'll never forget as long as I live.

"Oh, Derrick fuck me baby!"

"Yeah baby, who's pussy is this?"

"It's yours baby, all yours!"

"Give it to me baby!"

The door is open and Derrick and Lela are locked in each others arms. Her legs are wrapped around his waist. The scent of sex pervades the room. None of us can move. We just stand there in shock for a few seconds in disbelief. And then it happens. Taylor flips on the light switch.

"What the fuck?" yells Derrick.

They stop in motion and Derrick jumps off Lela and they both look towards the door. The expressions on their faces were worth a million dollars.

"Oh baby, it's not what you think. I can explain!" Derrick pleads as he's scrambling for his pants.

"I'm sorry Natalie," Lela says while wrapping the sheet around her. "I never meant…"

"You never meant what Lela? You never meant to fuck my man? You never meant for me to catch you? You never what?" I scream. She doesn't respond. Derrick walks towards me and tries to grab my arm. "Nat, let's go outside and talk," he says.

I jerk away from him. "Do not put your fucking hands on me! I cannot believe this shit! My best fucking friend! How could you Lela?" I am livid.

Lela leans against her dresser and starts to speak.

"Natalie, I'm sorry that you had to find out this way, but I love Derrick. I've loved him for a long time."

"You've loved Derrick for a long time? What the fuck does that mean?" I'm pissed.

"I mean that I am the person that Derrick was messing around with at Grambling. I'm the other woman. Michelle? That's me. Lela Michelle. I know that this is hurting you, but I'm tired of hiding and sneaking around." Lela has this attitude like I'm glad this shit is in the open. She shows no remorse.

"Be quiet Lela!" Derrick yells hysterically. "Natalie, let's go and talk."

Shaking my head. "No, no. Let's talk right here. Now it's all becoming clear. All the notes on your car at Grambling, all the gifts. Shit, why didn't I see it?" I ask.

"You low down maggot excuse of a woman. You ain't shit Lela, I need to beat your ass!" shouts Renee.

"Fuck you Renee!" Lela responds.

"No, fuck you!" Naomi says. "I don't know what your problem is but you're the one that's wrong and this apparent attitude that you're sporting is totally uncouth. How could you fuck your best friends man? Damn, that's low. With friends like you, give me all the fucking enemies in the world." Naomi explodes.

"How could you betray Natalie like this Lela? You are sick!" Taylor says as she wipes tears from her eyes.

"Will everyone calm down! Natalie can we please go somewhere and talk?" Derrick asks.

I turn towards him. "No Derrick we cannot go somewhere and talk. That's what got me caught up in you again. We are going to deal with this right here!"

'I ain't got time for this. I'm going to get me a cup of tea," Lela says arrogantly.

"Bitch, you ain't going nowhere." Naomi pushes Lela to the floor.

"You bitch!" Lela yells while scrambling with the sheet.

"I may be a bitch, but I ain't never slept with my best friends man. Now who's the real bitch?" Naomi asks.

"Fuck all of you. I don't know why all of you are in an uproar. Miss goody-two-shoes ain't all of that. We all know that she's been seeing Miles," says Lela.

"Yes, I was seeing Miles at first but you know that he and I haven't been together for months. However, this is not about Miles. This is about you and your betrayal," I say.

"Whatever! Get over it Natalie. Derrick and I love each other and that's that." She walks towards Derrick and he pushes her away.

"Lela, I don't love you. I love Natalie!" Derrick shouts.

"You weren't saying that earlier when you were fucking me!" Lela says sharply.

"Well, I'm telling you that I love Natalie."

"Ain't this a blip. You have some way of showing someone that you love them Derrick." Naomi interjects.

"I'm going to beat her ass for you!" Taylor says as she lunges towards Lela. I grab Taylor.

"Listen everyone. I can handle this." I reach into the depths of my soul and ask God to help me to stay calm. I realize that I'm dealing with two sick individuals, so I have to be the rational one. No tears for now. I take a deep breath and turn and look at Derrick. I begin speaking softly.

"Derrick, here we are again. Me hurt and you apologizing. Let me see, what was it that you said to me? Oh, babylove, I promise that I'll never hurt you again. I'm half a man without you. What was that about Derrick? More lies?"

"Nat, just let me explain."

"No, I don't want to hear it. I want you to stay the fuck out of my life. Act as if you've never heard of Natalie Norwood, because as of this moment I am erasing you from my mind completely. I never want to see you again. As far as I'm concerned, you're dead."

Looking at Lela, I feel tears welling in my eyes. The hurt I feel is indescribable.

"Lela, words will never be able to depict what I am feeling right now. I love you. You were like a sister to me. There is nothing on the face of this earth that I wouldn't do for you. To find out that you have been betraying me for all of these years is the most painful thing I've ever experienced. You've committed the worse act between friends. There is no explanation. I pity the both of you.

You deserve each other. And by the way, Lela wipe the cum off your mouth it's not very becoming." I turn and walk out of the room. My sisterfriends follow.

We all walk out of Lela's place with a piece of us gone. It really makes us question the whole aspect of friendship. How do you know if someone is really a true friend? If Lela could betray me, anyone can.

There is complete silence in the car except for the sound of my tears. I hurt beyond pain.

CHAPTER 33

Please God, let this be a dream. This type of pain could only exist in a dream. No one person could possibly contain this much pain inside. Why God? Why me? Have I done something so horrible in my life that I deserve to be hurting like this? No, I don't claim to be a saint, but I would never think of doing anything remotely close to what Lela pulled. Do you hear me God? I feel like dying. Death has to better than this. My best friend and my boyfriend. Who would have ever guessed.? I keep replaying last nights event in my mind and I just can't convince myself that it really happened. How did this happen? How could they have been messing around all of this time and I didn't see it? Am I that naïve? Or did I just choose to be blind? Have I really seen this all along? It doesn't matter. It happened and somehow I have got to get through this. How do I just move on without Lela and Derrick? We've shared so much. Shit, I guess that was a literal statement.

There's a knock at my bedroom door. It startles me at first until it dawns on me that my friends spent the night. They were adamant that I should not be alone in my condition.

"Come in," I say groggily.

Naomi pokes her head through the door. "Hi Nat, can we come in?"

"Sure, come on in," I say as I adjust my pillows and sit up. They all walk in very quietly and sit on my bed. The expressions on their faces say everything. I know that they are worried.

"So, how are you?" Renee asks.

"Horrible, pissed, hurt, disgusted. Shall I go on?" I ask.

"We are so sorry that this happened to you Natalie. You do not deserve this." Taylor says.

"I know, but it wasn't your fault. Lela and Derrick did this and right now I feel like someone has died. How could she do this to me? How could she?" Tears begin to flow fearlessly from my eyes. My body heaves and my breathing is jagged. Renee slides next to me and puts her arms around my shoulders.

"You're going to be just fine girl. It's going to be ok." She rocks me gently.

"No Renee, I won't. I'll never get over this. I just want to die!" I manage to say through the tears.

"Sweetie, you don't want to die. You're just hurting right now. Just wait. This too shall pass." Renee says softly.

"That's right Nat. You have so much to offer and we need you in our lives. We love you Nat and we're going to help you get through this." Naomi says while handing me a Kleenex from my nightstand.

"It hurts you guys," I whimper, "It really hurts."

"We know Nat, but we're here. We'll always be here for you." Taylor says. She and Naomi join Renee and wrap their arms around me. I close my eyes and give in to the pain. I feel my body trying to release this anguish, but it seems impossible to do.

CHAPTER 34

Several months have passed since the incident and I can't say that I feel any better. Not a single day has passed where I haven't cried or felt sick to my stomach. I feel as if I'm drowning and there is nothing that can save me. I'm trying desperately to immerse myself in my work, but that's not working either. I called Day and my sisterfriends last night and told them that I needed some space and that they wouldn't be hearing from me for a while. I need some time to get my thoughts in order. They all seemed to understand except for Day. She insisted that I come to Virginia, but I declined. My being in Virginia is not going to help this time. Nothing can help this situation.

Derrick has called me everyday trying to plead his case. He says that he loves me. Isn't that wonderful? He fucks my friend and through it all…he loves me. Last night there was a note on my car and the night before he was waiting outside my place. He looks like shit. I have never seen him look so bad, but he should have thought about that before he messed over me. Naomi says that she saw him a few days ago and he ran up to her begging her to talk to me for him. She said that she felt really bad for him especially after seeing him so depressed, but she thought of me and told him that he needed to go on with his life and under no circumstances would she talk to me on his behalf. He started crying and walked away. Well, good for him. He can cry a fucking river for all I care. Asshole. Dammit, why am I even thinking of him? Who cares if he's hurt? I'm hurting and I'm dealing with it. He can do the same. The phone rings.

"Newsroom. Natalie Norwood speaking."

"Natalie, please don't hang up. Please talk to me."

"Why are you calling me? Haven't I made myself perfectly clear? I have nothing to say to you." I try to keep my tone down . "I mean shit. Haven't you caused me enough pain?" I feel the tears about to come.

"Nat, baby just listen. I'm sorry! I need you in my life. I fucked up, but I'm begging you to give me another chance. Please baby, just meet me tonight and we can discuss this. Just one hour, that's all I'm asking for."

I pause slightly to get my words in order and instantaneously the words come to me: "Derrick listen to me and listen closely because I don't want to leave any room for miscommunication. I don't ever want to see you again. I don't ever want to talk to you again. As a matter fact, if you died this very moment, the world would be a better place. I cannot describe what I feel towards you. It's not hate, but rather I detest and pity you. And if that's not clear enough for you, I'll end this conversation with these final words: Stay the fuck out of my life!" I slam the phone down. Everyone in the newsroom turns towards me. I try and regain my composure, but the phone rings again.

"Hello!" I scream.

"Natalie, it's Frank."

"Oh, Frank. I'm sorry."

"Can you come to my office for a minute?" He asks in a very authoritative way.

Pausing slightly before answering, I say, "Sure, I'll be right there."

Why does Frank want to see me? I walk slowly towards his office, trying to linger in every step. I reach his door and stop. My heart starts to beat rapidly. I take a deep breath and knock on his door.

"Come in." Frank is standing and looking out of his window. His back is turned towards the door.

"Hi Frank."

"Have a seat Natalie," he says while still looking out of the window. "How are you Natalie?"

"Um, I'm fine Frank." I try to sound as confident and professional as ever. "Why do you ask?"

"Why do I ask Natalie?" He turns and just stares at me for a moment without saying a word.

"Frank, what's wrong?" I ask with my voice quivering. My nerves are getting the best of me.

"Can you honestly sit there and ask me what's wrong? I'll tell you what's wrong. You look like crap!" His tone startles me. "Forgive me, but I have to be honest with you. For months you have been going down hill. If it were not for Brad, the newscast would be shot to hell. Our ratings have been dropping and the staff has been complaining about your attitude."

"But Frank."

"No, listen to me Natalie. I like you. I hired you as the noon anchor because you're sharp and you have unlimited potential, but lately you haven't been yourself. There's no spark. I don't know what's going on with you, but you need to fix it." Frank finally sits down in his chair and leans towards me. "I want you to take a few weeks off."

"Frank, I don't."

Frank raises his hands.

"I've made my decision. You'll have 3 weeks off with pay." I must have looked completely dumbfounded.

"Yes, with pay," he says. "But when you return to work, I want to see the old Natalie. The Natalie I hired."

"I don't know what to say. I didn't know that things were this bad."

"Just get yourself together. Whatever is going on in your life needs to be dealt with and given closure. We all go through rough periods in our lives and some people handle it better than others. You'll be ok. Just remember that your news family cares."

"Thank you Frank, you don't know how much this means to me."

Smiling. "I think I do. By the way, your three weeks start today."

"But what about the newscast?"

"Brad can handle it."

"Okay."

"Natalie, don't look so sad. Your job will be waiting for you when you return. I promise."

"Thank you. I won't let you down." I turn to leave.

"Natalie, don't let yourself down."

"I hear you." I try to form a smile and walk out the door. I had no idea how this whole situation was affecting me at work. *Natalie, stop trippin', you know that you have not been yourself lately. Damn, I could have been fired.* This entire nightmare is out of control. I start gathering a few of my things at my desk and notice a Federal Express envelope in my mailbox. I slide it into the side pocket of my attache' case. I write Brad a quick note telling him that I'll see him in three weeks. It dawns on me that everyone in the newsroom is looking at me with this sort of pity in their eyes. I guess I have been on edge for a while. Before the tears start, I grab my things and rush to my car. As I'm walking out of the door, I nearly knock someone over in my haste to get out of the newsroom. It's Miles.

"Hey Nat." He looks at me intensely. "What's wrong?"

"Nothing," I say as I try to wipe the tears from my face.

Miles moves my hands and wipes my tears away with the bottom of his jacket. "Sweetheart, something is wrong. Do you want to talk about it?"

"No, I can't talk about anything right now!" I run to my car.

"Natalie!" Miles yells. I don't turn around. I get in my car and drive home. There, I don't look for a life jacket or a rope. I drown myself in my misery.

CHAPTER 35

I know that it's another day only because I see the sunlight seeping through my verticals. Here I am, day ten of my supposed healing period on the same couch and in the same pajamas. Drunk. I can't seem to pull myself out of this black hole of pain. Why me? Out of all of the people in this world, why me? I can feel the tears begin to well in my eyes again. My tear ducts should be dried up by now, but the tears keep coming. Tears of pain, tears of frustration, and most of all tears of heartbreak. My eyes hurt like hell. They are extremely swollen from all of this crying, but I haven't mustered up the courage to look in the mirror. I can't look at myself. It would only confirm what Frank said. I know that I look like shit. *Who cares? I don't.* I think I need another drink. My eyes focus in on the clock above the mantel. It's eight-o-clock. *A little early for a drink, huh Nat?* I ignore my inner voice and pour me another glass of rum. Pooch runs to the door and I let her out and decide to lie back on the couch. The phone rings and I just let the answering machine pick up. It's Day again. She's called 100 times. I specifically told Day and my sisterfriends that I needed some space, but do you think that any of them are respecting my wishes? No! Everyone wants to talk. Well, I don't. Miles called late last night and I started to pick up, but decided against it. I have to handle this on my on. I hear Pooch scratching at the door and let her in. Poor dog, I haven't played with her in days.

As I'm about to flop on the couch again, the phone rings. I decide to pick up this time.

"Hello."

"Were you sleep?" the voice asks.

"Uh, Miles?"

"Yeah, it's me."

"Why are you calling?" I ask.

"I just wanted to check on you. Are you ok?"

"I'm fine Miles." I try to speak convincingly.

"Well, can I go on record saying that I don't believe you?"

"Sure, you can believe whatever you want to believe," I say sarcastically.

"Natalie, I'm really worried about you. I saw Taylor today and she said that you weren't returning any of her calls. Your friends are worried too."

"Well, they shouldn't be. I just need my space. Can't anyone understand that?" I scream.

"Hey baby, I didn't mean to upset you. Maybe you should just call everyone and let them know that you're ok, just to put their minds at ease. They are just concerned like me."

"I know Miles, but I just can't deal with anyone right now. Can you understand?" I start to cry.

"Sweetheart, I do understand. How about I call Taylor and the crew and let them know that you're ok?"

"Thank you Miles."

"Natalie?"

"Yes."

"I'm here if you need me."

"I know."

"Bye."

"Bye Miles."

I hang up the phone, finish my drink and drift back into a deep sleep. I dream that I'm being pushed off of a cliff and just before I fall I get a glimpse at who has pushed me. It's Lela and Derrick. They're laughing hysterically. When I wake up my pajamas are clinging to my body, soaked from perspiration. My stomach is in knots. I pour another drink and feel my body relax.

CHAPTER 36

Obviously I think that I am still dreaming when I hear someone knocking at the front door. It doesn't dawn on me that it isn't a dream until Pooch starts barking. Slurring my words, "Pooooooch, whuz wrong?" Pooch continues to bark.

"Natalie! Open the door! I know that you're in there. It's me Miles."

The voice echoes from the other side of the door. I'm trying desperately to get my thoughts in order, but I am totally disoriented.

"Miles?" I say in a barely audible whisper. "What are you doing here?" I say while trying to get up from the sofa. However, my body just isn't cooperating. Damn, my head hurts and my stomach feels as if it's boiling.

"Natalie, I am not leaving until you open this door!" He pounds away.

"Please stop that knocking." I want to yell, but nothing comes out. Why doesn't everyone just leave me alone? I finally get my body to cooperate a little bit. I roll off the couch and fall flat on my face, but at least I'm off of the couch. Since I can't possibly stand, I crawl slowly to the door. Pooch is looking at me as if I've lost my mind. Who knows? Maybe I have. Using every ounce of strength that I have, I reach for the lock and open the door. As the door opens, I collapse again. Only this time I fall on Miles' feet.

"What the hell! Natalie, oh my God!" Miles yells as he kneels down on the floor beside me and holds me in his arms. "Oh baby, what's happening to you?" he asks while rubbing my back. He lifts my chin and I try to open my eyes more, but I can't. I feel really sick. I need to go to the bathroom. Lord, please help me get up. Before I can even get that thought out I throw up all over Miles. The stench is unbearable. "Miiiiiiles, I'm soooooo sorry."

"It's okay, let's get you cleaned up," he says and lifts me up from the floor. Miles carries me into the bathroom and lays me on the rug. He opens the shower door and turns the water on. Slowly and ever so gently he begins to take my pajamas off. I know that I must smell horrible. I haven't bathed in days. Miles doesn't say a word. After he has undressed me, he begins to take his clothes off.

"Miiiiiiles what are?"

"Shhhhhh. Come on," he says while helping me into the shower.

Miles positions me so that the water hits me directly. The water is very hot, but it feels good against my skin. He holds me in his arms and just lets me rest my head against his chest for a few moments. "I'm gonna bathe you okay?" he asks while lifting my head. I nod yes.

Miles takes my facecloth and wipes my face. Then he reaches for my bath sponge and pours some gel on it and begins to lather my body. He scrubs every inch of my body with an overpowering sense of gentleness. He then sits me down on the bench inside of my shower and gets on his knees. Pulling both of my legs towards him, he places my feet on his stomach, reaches for my razor and begins to shave my legs. *Now, what man do you know would think to do something like this? Only Miles.* Afterwards, he washes my hair. I'm starting to feel better.

Miles dries me off and lotions me down. I finally look in the mirror. "I look bad huh?" I ask.

"No, you're beautiful." He says while rubbing a towel through my hair.

"You just don't want to hurt my feelings," I say.

"Natalie, you're always going to be beautiful to me. Now, why don't you sit down and I'll blow dry your hair. Where do you keep your blow dryer?"

"Here," I say while pulling my drawer open.

Miles combs my tangles out and begins to dry my hair. This feels really good. I've always liked someone else doing my hair. Once my hair is dried, I brush my teeth and slip into a pair of fresh pajamas. Miles helps me into bed.

"Get some rest Nat, and I'll be here when you wake up."

"Miles."

"Yeah."

"Thank you."

"Don't mention it." He leans towards me and kisses me on the cheek. "Good night."

"Good night," I say as I watch him walk out of the bedroom. I fall asleep. This time no nightmares.

CHAPTER 37

I open my eyes slowly and stare at the ceiling. Within a few minutes I finally decide to sit up. To my surprise no headache or nausea. I make my way to the bathroom and as I'm about to wash my face I take a long look at myself in the mirror. *A little better than last night, but not much. What's happening to you Natalie?* I quickly wash my face and brush my teeth and head to the kitchen. I open my bedroom door and to my surprise Miles is still here.

"Good morning," he says.

"Miles, you're still here," I say.

"Now where else would I be?" he asks while pouring a glass of apple juice. "Are you hungry?"

"Uh, not really. But I'll take some toast."

"Coming up," he says while smiling and placing two slices of bread in the toaster.

Miles hands me the glass of juice as I sit down.

"How are you feeling Nat?" he asks while grabbing a small plate for the toast.

"I feel pretty good."

"That's good to hear. I was really worried about you last night," he says while sitting next to me.

"You didn't have to stay Miles."

"I wanted to. Besides, I've taken a few days off and I thought that we could hang out."

"Mmmm, I don't know. I just really need some time alone," I say while taking a sip of juice.

"Time alone had you in a drunken stupor," he says sarcastically. "Time alone is not what you need. You need to get yourself together so that you can be the productive and beautiful woman that you are, and not sitting around this apartment feeling sorry for yourself. You're not the first person to have someone cheat on them."

His last line stung like a wasp. I detected a slight bit of anger but he didn't let it really show.

"How do you know what happened? Who have you talked to?" I ask in total shock.

"Natalie," Miles says while leaning on his elbows, "Vegas is small and word gets around fast. I know that Derrick slept with Lela. The whole situation is fucked up, but you have got to move on."

I get up from the table and walk towards the kitchen sink. "Miles, you don't understand and I know that you're trying to help but I'd appreciate it if you just stepped off. This is none of your business." My voice raises slightly and I can feel myself tensing up. Without looking at him I say, "Miles, I think that you should leave." There is silence for a few seconds and then Miles walks towards me and puts his arms around me.

"Natalie, I'm not going anywhere. I am not leaving you alone."

"But I want you to go! I want everyone to leave me the fuck alone!" I scream.

He turns me around and grabs my shoulders. "No! No, Natalie, I will not leave you alone. You are going to snap out of this!"

"I don't want to snap out of it! Don't you understand?" I say while pounding fearlessly on his chest. Miles just lets me hit him over and over again until I just break into tears.

"It's okay babe. I'm here," he says softly while holding me in his arms.

"Miles, it hurts so bad. When will it stop? When, Miles?" I cry out.

"The pain will leave baby. You're going to be just fine. You'll get through this." Miles continues to hold me until it's all out.

We sit back down at the table and I tell him the whole story. I feel a sense of relief being able to express my true feelings about this horrible ordeal. Miles listens intently, but never says a word. Afterwards, we get dressed and take a walk. We hold hands in silence while I allow the sun to energize my body. Almost miracle like, I feel my body responding to the rays and a small voice inside me whispers that everything will be alright.

CHAPTER 38

My three weeks off with pay is almost over. I have two more days left and its back to the newsroom. I can't wait! I must admit that I've missed the hustle and bustle of everyday drama. However, these three weeks have done me a world of good. Not to mention the presence of Miles. He has been absolutely wonderful. We've seen each other every day and not once has he mentioned the Derrick incident. I must have a guardian angel looking over me because the average brotha would not have a thing to do with me, but not Miles. He hasn't skipped a beat. We drove to Disneyland a few days ago and just spent the day being big kids and today we've decided that we're going to grill some steaks at his place and spend the day indoors. What's amazing is that we haven't made love. Most men would have jumped at the opportunity to take advantage of someone in my position, but not Mr. Grey. Miles has been absolutely wonderful. Not that I haven't had the urge, but it's been nice just spending quality time with Miles without the sex. Don't get me wrong, that man has the penis of a god, but I just needed some time to fully close that recent chapter in my life.

I stopped at home to get a change of clothes and to get some more dog food for Pooch. Yes, Pooch has been with us too. As I'm packing some things in my overnight bag, I notice a Federal Express envelope lying on my chaise. It dawns on me that that is the envelope that I received right before my leave. I walk towards my chair and pick it up. There's no return address. Mmmmm, that's strange. I sit down and open the envelope. I recognize the handwriting immediately-it's Lela's. My stomach becomes uneasy. I take a few deep breaths and begin reading the letter:

Dear Natalie,

I am probably the last person that you expected to hear from. I really don't know where to begin. I know that I hurt you in the worst way possible by committing the unspeakable between friends. I never meant to hurt you Natalie and I hope that you believe that, but part of me has always been jealous of you. You are so pretty and smart and guys are always flocking towards you. The day that we saw Derrick in front of the Student Union and Grambling, I wanted him with all of my heart, but he wanted you. I couldn't stand it. Why did all of the fine guys always want you?

I was attractive and smart and yet you always prevailed. Every since we were kids, you were first at everything: first at spelling bees, track meets and beauty pageants. There I was trailing behind your glory. Well, I promised myself that once we got to Grambling you were not ever going to beat me again and so I pursued Derrick. At first he resisted, but eventually my money changed his mind. Remember, how you use to always question where did Derrick get the money to dress so well? Well, I was buying his clothes. And that new car that he popped up with in his senior year? Yes, I purchased that too. All of your suspicions in college were right. You just didn't know that it was me the entire time. I hate to admit this, but your pain brought me pleasure. I now know that my actions were wrong and that my thinking was sick. You have been nothing but a loving friend my entire life and this is how I repay you. I am so sorry Natalie. I know that I will never find another friend like you. I hope that you'll be able to forgive me one day. Please give my apologies to the Sisterfriends. I realize that I hurt them too. For the record, I haven't heard from Derrick. The last time we spoke he was entirely distraught over losing the one woman that he loved. And it wasn't me. By the time you get this letter I will be in Chicago. I have accepted a new position with a non-profit organization. Take care of yourself and again, I am so very very sorry.

Lela

I close my eyes for a moment and let what I just read sink in. I am in shock and yet a part of me still hurts. Flashes of my childhood appear. I can't remember a time when Lela was not a part of my life. How can this be? How could Lela have had all of these mixed feelings towards me? This is too deep. I don't know if I should feel anger or a sense of relief. I take a deep breath and feel a tear roll down my cheek. I calmly say out loud, "Natalie, this too shall pass. It's over. Let it go." I put the letter back in the envelope, grab my lighter and burn her words.

CHAPTER 39

It only takes me a few minutes to get to Miles' place. I take out my compact and check my face to make sure that I don't look like I've been crying, but I do. Oh well, such is life. I knock on the door and hear Pooch barking. Miles opens the door smiling.

"That was quick," he says as I walk through the door.

"Yeah, I didn't have a whole lot to get," I say while sitting my things down.

Miles walks up behind me and puts his arms around me. "What's wrong baby? And don't say nothing, cuz I see it all in your eyes." I turn to face him, "I got a letter from Lela and it just really upset me." I walk towards the couch, sit down and run my fingers through my hair and gently massage my temples.

"What did the letter say?" Miles asks.

"She apologized for hurting me and hopes that one day I will forgive her," I say.

"Will you?"

"Will I what?" I ask.

"Will you ever forgive her for what she did?"

Leaning back on the sofa, I think for a moment before I answer Miles. "Honey, I'm sure that I will. I know that I cannot move forward until I forgive them both. However, I don't know if I will ever be able to be friends with Lela again. What she did to me cut to the core. I could never trust her."

"I understand babe. It will take some time, but once you've fully forgiven them both and release it completely, you'll have peace."

"And how did you become so wise?" I ask while scooting towards him.

"Living! It'll do it to you every time." We both laugh. I lean over and plant a soft kiss on Miles' lips.

"Mmmm, what's that for?" he asks while pulling me closer.

"Just wanted to say thank you," I say.

"For what?" he asks.

"Just for being a wonderful man. You are truly a blessing in my life."

"And you are mine," he says while holding me close. Something magical starts to happen in this moment. I feel our hearts connecting. The beat is becoming one.

CHAPTER 40

As we're pulling into Albertson's, I grab the grocery list and scan over it once more.

"Miles, are you sure this is all we need?" I ask.

"Yeah, that should be enough," he replies while opening his car door. "Maybe I'll grab some fresh shrimp while we're in here. You ready?" He gets out and walks around to the passenger side to let me out. We grab hands and walk towards the grocery store, but before we can get inside we pause for second at the sight before us. It's Derrick, and he looks really bad. Miles grabs my hand tighter.

"You okay?" he asks with a deep concern.

"Uh, yeah. I'm fine," I say while Derrick and I lock eyes.

I knew that this was inevitable. Derrick and I would bump heads sooner or later. I was hoping for later. God, he looks like death. He's gotten so thin. What happened to his hair? We're approaching Derrick slowly. He speaks.

"Hello, Natalie." He pauses slightly. "Hey man, what's up?" he says while looking at Miles. Miles and I both say, "Hello."

"Uh, is it ok if I speak to you for a moment Natalie?" Derrick asks in a very humbling way.

"I don't…"

"Listen Natalie, I'm not going to harass you. I just want to talk to you for a moment," he pleads.

"You don't have to do this!" Miles says while stepping in front of me.

"Miles, it's ok. I'll be fine. Why don't you go on inside. Here's the list and I'll be in shortly," I say, while handing him the grocery list.

"You sure?" he asks.

"Yes," I say convincingly.

Miles kisses me softly on the lips and walks off. Derrick and I walk over to a bench outside of the store and take a seat.

"So, how have you been Natalie?"

"I've been fine Derrick. And yourself?" I ask while really getting a good look at him. This isn't the Derrick that I knew. Something is going on.

"I've been better," he says while rubbing his hands together. Derrick turns and looks and me and then grabs my hand. I don't snatch it away. Something tells me that I need to just stay calm. "Natalie, first of all I want to say that I'm sorry."

"Derrick, you don't need…"

"Shhh, let me finish." He lets go of my hand and leans back on the bench. "I hurt you. No, I fucked over you in the worse way possible and saying I'm sorry isn't enough. You are a wonderful woman and you may not believe this, but I do love you and I always will." He pauses for a second and shifts slightly. "I don't have any excuses for what happened between Lela and myself. I simply got caught up in the game and to be perfectly honest, I never thought I would get caught. Not me, not Derrick Foster." He laughs to himself. "But every player has his day. I had all the intention in the world of settling down with you. I guess I just never grew up. It's hard to admit these things. The truth really hurts." I notice tears forming in his eyes.

"Derrick, are you okay?"

"Yeah, I'm fine. Just give me a moment." He wipes his eyes and continues.

"Nat, please know that I never meant to hurt you. I wish that I could go back to the first day that I laid eyes on you. You were so beautiful and so kind. In all the years that we were involved, you gave me nothing but love and I gave you nothing but pain. I am sorry with all of my heart." He pauses again and looks at me. Nothing could have prepared me for what came out his mouth next. "Natalie, I have lung cancer."

"Oh, Derrick. I am so sorry." I say while trying to keep my emotions under control.

"Well, the doctor's have only given me a year to live and I had to make sure that I saw you. I needed you to know how I felt."

"Derrick, I don't know what to say."

"Just say that one day you'll forgive me. I'm not saying that it has to be today, but one day I hope that you can." Derrick takes a handkerchief out of his pocket and wipes his eyes. I grab his hands.

"Derrick, I don't even know where to begin. I loved you so much and all I ever wanted was for you to love me and respect me in the same way. Each day that passes I find myself get stronger and stronger. I have to admit, catching you in bed with my best friend hurt beyond words. I will never be able to forget that, but I have moved on. It's strange that I would run into you today. I got a letter of apology from Lela and she said almost the same thing that you said. That she never meant to hurt me. Well, what did the two of you think would happen to me when I found out? The two of you can't be that naïve." I take a deep breath. "Listen, I've closed that chapter of my life. I really don't hold any hostility towards either of you. Yeah, it still hurts a bit, but soon that will fade too. I'm sorry about your health and I will keep you in my prayers. At this very moment I can't say when I'll be able to forgive you. I am working very hard to get to that point, but right now it's still too fresh in my mind." I see Miles coming out of the door.

"Natalie, I wish you the best that life has to offer. If anyone deserves happiness you do." We stand up and embrace. I feel the tears rolling down my face.

"Take care of yourself," I whisper in his ear.

"I love you Natalie Norwood," he whispers back. I walk towards Miles and we head to the car. He doesn't ask any questions. As we pull off I get one last look at Derrick. One last look at an old love. All of a sudden, something tells me that I need to forgive Derrick right now. I can't keep this grudge in my heart and I can't just not grant him a final wish from me.

As we drive past the bench where he is sitting, I look at him through the window and mouth, "I forgive you." He smiles and says, "Thank you." *I remember the first day that I saw him. Oh, that smile melted my heart. I laugh to myself and remember that there were some good times with him.* I reach over and grab Miles' hand. We drive home in silence and without saying a word we both know that this incident marks the closing of an old chapter and the beginning of a new. Ours.

CHAPTER 41

When Miles and I get to his apartment, I tell him about the conversation between Derrick and I. Afterwards, I go into the bedroom and lie down. I find myself crying a gut-wrenching cry. It seems as if a part of me has died. I can't remember not loving Derrick and now he's dying. I never anticipated this. I mean, I thought we would just simply go our separate ways and maybe bump into one another every blue moon, but not death. I close my eyes and pray for Derrick. I even say a prayer for Lela and before I know it, laughter awakens me.

I didn't realize I fell asleep. I crawl out of bed and go into the bathroom to freshen up.

I wonder who's here? I walk out of the bedroom and am greeted by the best presents in the world.

"Hey girl, we thought you were going to sleep your life away." Taylor says while embracing me.

"You guys, what are you doing here?" A big smile takes over my face.

"Shoot, you wouldn't come to us, so we had to come and check on our girl," Naomi says while joining in on the hug.

"We love you Nat," says Renee. We stand there holding each other for a few moments.

"Hey, can't your Sister Dear get some love?" Day yells while coming out of the kitchen holding a bowl of spinach dip.

"Oh, Sister Dear!" I scream. "What is going on?" Day gives me the warmest embrace and kisses me on the cheek.

"Sister, you've had enough space and time. Now it's time to move on. Agree?"

"I agree. Now tell me how you guys knew I was here." Everyone smiles and turns toward Miles.

"Honey, you did this?" I ask.

"It was nothing. I thought it was time for you to be with your sister and your girls."

"That was so sweet. Thank you." I kiss him lightly on the lips.

"Well, I'm outta here," Miles says while grabbing his gym bag.

"Babe, where are you going?" I ask.

"I'm gonna play some ball with the boys and I'll be back later on. The food is ready. You all enjoy yourself."

"Bye Miles," everyone says in unison.

"Later," he says as I walk him to the door. "Honey, thank you. This is so wonderful of you."

"Anything for you," Miles says while grabbing me in his arms and planting one of those sugar daddy kisses on me.

"See ya later," I say.

"You can count on it."

I stand at the door and watch Miles as he pulls off. I close the door and everyone that I love is smiling at me.

"What?" I ask dumbfounded.

"You know what. That man was about to eat you up," Renee says while grabbing a handful of chips.

"You are crazy," I say casually while not being able to hide my true feelings.

"Yeah, it's gone be some fuckin' goin' on here tonight," Taylor says.

We all laugh. I had forgotten how much I had missed everyone. This is true happiness.

The smell of hickory permeates the room. We all fix our plates and sit outside on the patio. I grab the bottle of Kendall Jackson Chardonnay and pour a glass for each of us.

"So girl, how have you been?" Naomi asks while cutting into her steak.

"I've been good. It was really hard at first, but things are getting better," I say.

"Miles told us about Derrick. How do you feel about that?" Day pauses for a moment. "I mean that's some deep shit."

"I don't really know how I feel. Of course it saddens me to know that someone I loved so much is dying, but I still have to deal with the whole Lela crap."

"Have you heard from Lela since the incident?" asks Renee.

"Yeah, she wrote me a letter apologizing for hurting me and then she went on to say that she had been jealous of me ever since we were kids."

Day quickly butts in, "I told you a while ago that Lela has always been jealous of you and that you needed to watch yourself around her."

"I know Day, but God! Who would have guessed that my best friend would betray me like this?" I say while peeling a shrimp and dipping it in the melted butter.

"Girrrrl, that's who'll do it to you. Your friends." Taylor licks her finger. "Not us, but there are some scandalous heifers out there. We just didn't pick up on that shit with Lela."

"I heard that she left town. Is that true?" Renee asks.

"She took a position in Chicago with some non-profit agency." I say as I lean back and rub my neck.

"Good riddance! Enough about that whole episode." Day says while reaching for a piece of corn. "Let's talk about something good, like you and Miles!" We all laugh.

"That's right! Give us the scoop on Mr. Miles. Have you given him any? Naomi asks in her normal nonchalant way.

"Not yet. We've been taking it slow. He's a good man." I don't realize that I'm blushing.

"Now that's the look that you used to have when you talked about Miles." Taylor says while giving me a soft nudge.

"I know. I know. I keep wondering how things would be between Miles and I had I not gone back to Derrick."

"Well, you may not like what I'm about to say." Day takes a sip of her wine and looks me in the eye. "You needed to resolve your feelings with Derrick. Even though things turned out bad, you needed to know if there was anything there. If you had not given Derrick another chance, you would have always wondered what if. Now you know and you can go on with your life."

"I agree with Day," Renee says. "It never would have worked for you and Miles if you had all of these unanswered questions regarding you and Derrick.

"I just feel like such a fool."

"Girl join the party!" Taylor exclaims. "We have all made mistakes when it comes to men. And the good thing about it is that you don't have to be a fool for life."

"I know that's right girl!" Naomi says while giving Taylor a high five.

I walk towards the grill and place a piece of salmon on my plate. "Well, I'm just glad it's over. Now, you guys need to bring me up to date on your lives."

We spend the rest of the afternoon laughing and catching up on everything. Through a majority vote it is decided that I needed to sweep the cobwebs out of my coochie. So, we pile into Renee's car and head to Victoria's Secret to get me something sexy for tonight. *"Well Natalie, it's time for the old you to emerge. Tonight is the night to get things back on track."* I say to myself while blushing. I feel myself getting a little excited. All of a sudden I can see Miles' beautiful penis. *Damn, it's been too long.*

CHAPTER 42

M iles arrives home to a barely lit apartment. Several candles are placed around the room and a trail of rose petals lead from the front door to the bedroom. He calls out my name, I don't answer. I hear him walking towards the bedroom. I must admit, I'm a little nervous. It feels like the first night that Miles and I were together. Miles pushes the door open and follows the trail of petals to the bathroom.

"Hello," he says while placing his gym bag down and kneels next to the tub.

"Hi Babe," I reply as I sink further into the tub of bubbles. Miles starts to run his fingers through my hair.

"So, what's this about?" he asks while giving me this devilish smile.

"What's what about?" I ask coyly.

Miles moves closer and lets his hand slide beneath the bubbles and starts to gently caress my breasts. "What's this about?" he asks again while forming tiny circles with his fingertips around my nipples. I feel my body responding to his touch.

"Mmmm, I just wanted to welcome you back home after a hard day of basketball," I say with a chuckle.

"This is some kind of welcome," he says while letting his hand move down my stomach to my navel.

"You deserve it. You've been so kind and loving towards me and I don't know if I'll ever be able to make up for the pain I've caused you." I sit up and place my hand on his face. "Miles, I am so sorry for everything." I kiss him softly on his nose. He smiles.

"Listen Nat, there is no need to apologize. We all make mistakes and hopefully we learn a valuable lesson from each. Let's just put the past aside and move forward, but before we do that I need to know something."

"What is it?"

"Are you ready for this?" Miles asks while pulling me up from the hot water.

"Yes, I am," I say softly.

"Are you sure? Because it's do or die from this point on?"

"I've never been more sure of anything in my life." I say as a tear rolls down my face.

"What's wrong Nat?"

"It's just that I could have lost you forever and…"

"Shhhh, don't even go there. You have me. That is if you want me?"

I let myself lean into his body. I breathe in his clean scent and I kiss him like I've never kissed him before.

"Does that answer your question?"

"I'm still not sure. Just a sec." Miles takes off his clothes and steps into the tub and pulls me down on top of him. I straddle him slowly allowing my sugar walls to feel every inch of him. I start to move up and down his rod and I hear him moan. *Forget the foreplay, my stuff is screaming.*

"Miles Grey?"

"Yes."

"I want you and I need you in my life."

He grabs my ass and pulls me closer. I feel his hardened rod go deeper inside of me and I shiver in delight.

"I'm yours," he growls. We kiss again and just hold each other in silence for a moment. Miles lifts me out of the water and sits me on his face while he softly teases my little friend with his tongue. Damn, this man has an incredible tongue. I squeeze his head with my thighs. I feel his finger go inside me. He finds the ultimate spot and begins to play with it while still sucking and licking my clit. I scream. My body becomes weak and I feel my sweet juices flowing. I kiss him and become even more turned on by my taste on his tongue. I plunge underwater and suck his rod until he explodes. *I'll share my secret later.* Afterwards, we relish in the moment and then bathe each other slowly. As we're drying off, Miles turns me towards the mirror and leans me against the sink. I feel him against my butt and I know that he's ready again.

"You ready for Daddy to really spank that ass?"

"Ohh, Daddy!" We both laugh and then he grabs my hips and takes me to our own secret place. Our own dark, wet, hot, secret place. I allow my body to open up completely to him. Our souls connect. This time it's so right.

CHAPTER 43

My heart beats rapidly as I step out of my car. It's my first day back to work since my leave of absence. Boy, am I nervous. I grab my briefcase and walk towards the door while slowly taking deep breaths. "I'm ready for this," I say to myself. I open the door to the newsroom and see brightly colored balloons everywhere. I wonder whose birthday it is?

"Surprise!" Rhonda yells as she walks from around the corner with the rest of the staff.

"Welcome back Natalie, we've missed you," Brad says while kissing me on the cheek.

"Oh, you guys! You didn't have to do this."

"Yes, we did. Girl, we need you to do some work around here." Rhonda jokes while giving me a tight hug. "I'm so glad to see you," she whispers in my ear.

"Me too," I say and notice that our general manager has just walked through the door.

"Natalie, I see that you're back." He extends his hand.

"Yes sir, I am," I say while shaking his hand firmly.

"Well good. I look forward to seeing you and Brad today."

"Thank you Mr. Hawkins." I pause slightly. "Thank you for everything."

"Don't mention it, just make the station proud."

"You got it."

Frank walks out of the newsroom and everyone makes their way towards me and welcomes me back. I feel a great since of care in this room and it feels wonderful. Considering all of the horrible emotions that I've experienced in these past months, this feels great. I talk to Brad and my news director for a few moments about today's newscast and then head to my desk where the most beautiful exotic arrangement is sitting. I quickly grab the card.

Welcome back, I know that you'll do well.
Miles
P.S. I can still feel you…

I can feel myself about to start blushing uncontrollably. I place the card in my briefcase and notice a wave of warmth over my body. *Natalie, now is not the time to be thinking about Big Daddy. I smile at the thought.* I look at the stack of papers on my desk and thank God for this moment and for helping me get back on track. Natalie Norwood the afternoon anchorwoman is back.

ONE YEAR LATER

CHAPTER 44

"Infertile couples spend thousands of dollars every year trying to get pregnant, often with no luck. Well, there's help on the way. We'll tell you about a new drug that's being tested in England. That story plus Matt's unsung hero coming up today at five."

"Thanks, for joining us. Have a great afternoon."

"That's it guys. Great show."

"Thanks Rob," I say while grabbing my scripts.

"Did you see the ratings?" Brad asks.

"Yeah, can you believe it? I mean, we're beating Channel 8 and 13."

"No, we're kickin' 8 and 13's asses," Brad laughs as I give him a high five.

"I didn't want to go there, but heeeeey!" I snap my fingers.

"Natalie, you are crazy."

"But really Brad, it just feels good to be at the top of my game. We are a great team and to be perfectly honest, I wasn't sure if we were going to cut it. I never said anything, but I was nervous as hell when they offered me this position with my limited experience."

"Natalie, the big guy saw some real talent and didn't want it to get by. I saw it in you the first day that we met. It was in your eyes." He motions to his eyes. "They had fire and you could just see your eagerness to be the best that you could be."

"I just can't believe that my dream has come to fruition."

"This is only the beginning. Step one of the dream." He holds up one finger. "Do you understand?"

"Yeah."

"You hungry?"

"I'm starving."

"Let's go to Formosa's."

"That's all you had to say, I'm following you."

Brad and I gather all of our things and head to lunch.

CHAPTER 45

Brad and I have a wonderful lunch together. I've become really good friends with Brad and his wife Kathy, which is quite surprising to me. Considering that I've never really had a true friendship with a white person. The unique thing about it is that Brad and Kathy have truly made an effort to be friends. There have been nights when we've had serious dialogue about race relations and instead of becoming defensive at every comment, they have really done some true soul searching. I have also had to take a serious look at how I view white people collectively. I can honestly say that Brad and Kathy are beautiful people and are a constant reminder to me that people are people no matter what their skin color. A few weeks ago they attended a Kwaanza celebration with Miles and I. Brad and Kathy were the only white faces in the crowd, but you never noticed it because they just fit right in. They were dancing and singing and to my surprise they both have a little rhythm. My phone startles my thought.

"News channel 4, this is Natalie."

"Natalie Norwood?" The voice inquires.

"Yes it is." I say with a little hesitation not recognizing the voice.

"Miss Norwood, my name is Dr. Hugh Jacobs. I'm the chief of oncology at Rainbow Medical Center."

"How can I help you Dr. Jacobs?"

"Well, a patient of mine has asked me to call you."

"A patient?" I ask.

"Yes, a Mr. Derrick Foster."

"Derrick!" I exclaim.

"Yes. Derrick has been in my care for several months and his condition has worsened. I don't expect him to make it through the week. The cancer is spreading and his health is deteriorating rapidly." There's complete silence. I'm trying to say something but the words just seem to be locked inside. I hear what the doctor is saying, but I can't believe it. I knew that Derrick had cancer, but I just figured that he would beat it. Oh, God.

"Miss Norwood?"

"Uh, yeah."

"Are you okay?" he asks with a deep air of concern.

"I'm sorry. What did you say?" My mind is races a mile a minute.

"I was asking if you're okay."

"Yeah, I'm fine Dr. Jacobs." I feel the tears about to well and I try my hardest to prevent that from happening.

"Well, the reason that I'm calling is that Derrick would like to see you."

"See me?"

"Yes, today if possible."

"Today?"

"As I mentioned Miss Norwood, we don't expect him to make it to the end of the week." I'm sure this doctor has had to say this a thousand times, but I am having a hard time grasping all of this at once.

"Uh, today huh?"

"Is that a problem?"

"No! I'll stop by today."

"Thank you Miss Norwood, I'm sure Derrick will appreciate this."

"You're welcome."

"Bye now." The doctor hangs up and I just sit at my desk listening to a dial tone until the loud beeping snaps me out of my zone. *Lord Jesus, I can't handle this right now? Natalie you cannot break down at work. Finish your assignments and then deal with everything else tonight. Yeah right. How am I supposed to concentrate after this?* I grab a tissue and walk outside. I see Miles pulling into the garage. I walk towards the van.

"Hi babe."

"Hey beautiful. What's wrong? You look like you've been crying." Miles wipes my eyes with his fingers.

I look up at him and start to tell him that Derrick is in the hospital and before I know it, I just break down into tears. Miles doesn't say a word. He just holds me until I get my composure. A few minutes later I am able to tell him everything. He asks if I would like for him to come with me to the hospital, but I tell him that I need to do this alone. He says that he understands and that he'll be at home if I need him.

CHAPTER 46

As I walk through the automatic doors of Rainbow Medical Center, I am immediately hit by that familiar hospital smell. That smell that turns my stomach and puts fear in my gut. I try to ignore it as I walk up to the receptionist and inquire as to what room Derrick Foster is in. She looks down the hospital roster and tells me that he's down the hall in room 639. For some reason my feet feel heavy and my pace has slowed. What am I going to see when I walk into room? I've been trying to prepare myself but I have to admit that I'm scared. This is someone that I loved with all of my heart and now he's dying. How do I handle this? I have never imagined Derrick not being around. Even if we were not together, I always knew that he was just a phone call away. And as much pain as he brought me, I still feel as if a huge part of me is being stripped away.

I stop at the room and just stare at the numbers on the door for a moment as if something magical is about to happen. I take a deep breath and knock on the door. No one answers, so I turn the doorknob slowly and walk in. The blinds are drawn so the room is dark with the exception of the light coming from the television. I see Derrick. Even in the darkness, I can see his frailty. I walk towards him and take a seat in the chair next to his bed. His eyes are closed. He's bald, no doubt from the chemo treatments that he's been receiving. I reach over and turn the bedside lamp on and just stare at him for a moment. Derrick seems to have lost all of his coloring. I feel myself welling up as I look at him attached to all of this equipment. He seems so helpless. I reach for his hand and begin to softly rub my palm over his. He opens his eyes. There is no life in them.

"Nat, is that you?" His voice is barely audible.

"Uh huh, yeah, it's me." A tear falls on my hand.

"I'm glad that you came."

"Oh, Derrick!" I can't control my tears.

"Shhh, don't cry Nat. Don't be sad," He says while trying to lift himself, but he's far too weak. I softly press upon his chest.

"Don't move, I'm ok." I wipe the tears from my face. "Do you want me to get you something?"

"Just help me to sit up a bit."

I lift his body and fluff the pillows for him. I cannot believe how much weight Derrick has lost. "Is that better?" I ask.

"Yeah, that's fine," Derrick says while grabbing my hand.

"Natalie, I love you."

"Listen Derrick, there's no need for you to go into all of this."

"No Natalie. It is important." He begins to cough and I hold a glass of water up to his lips to drink.

"Derrick, it's really ok," I say as I place the glass back on the bed stand.

"Let me talk Natalie. I only have a few hours left on this earth and need to say this!"

"Derrick, don't say that. You never know what can happen," I say pleadingly.

"No Natalie. I've accepted my fate. At first I was devastated. To be perfectly honest, I was scared as hell, but I'm fine now." He pauses and takes a few deep breaths. "I know that I haven't always done the right thing, but I have had a good life. Meeting you was the highlight of my life. You taught me about true love. I just never fully appreciated you. I want you to know that you're a beautiful woman and that my life has been blessed from knowing and loving you."

"Derrick, why now? Why?" I get up and start pacing the floor.

"Because I want you to know that it wasn't your fault. It wasn't you. It was me. I know that there have been times when I made you doubt your self-worth and I just want you to know that I was just messed up. I thought that running around on you was the macho thing to do. I knew that you were a good woman. Shit, I was the envy on campus. Like so many men, I wanted to be a playa and I was until everything hit the fan. I got in over my head." Derrick begins to cry a deep painful cry. The kind of cry that makes your body shake. "Damn it Natalie, I'm dying and I can't change a thing. I can't start all over with you. I wish that I could. I would treasure you. Nat, baby I am so sorry."

"Don't cry. It's going to be ok. Shhh. I'm here with you." I rub his shoulder until he stops crying. I grab a tissue and wipe the tears from his thin face. "Derrick, I really don't know what to say other than I've forgiven you. We were young back then and the recent mess is really water under the bridge. It has all been a learning process. Don't beat yourself up over what has been. I don't hold any hard feelings towards you."

I lean towards him and give him a soft kiss on the lips. "You were the first man that I loved. Don't ever forget that okay? And everything wasn't bad. We've had some wonderful moments." I touch his face and really take in this moment. Something in my soul tells me that this is the last time that I'll be seeing Derrick.

"I have to go now," I say while reaching for my purse.

"Nat?"

I turn and look back at Derrick. "I love you."

"Me too." I say while trying to hold back the tears. I walk out into the hall, lean on the wall and fall to the floor. Too many emotions float around inside my head. "God, please don't let him die," I whisper, "He doesn't deserve to die. He's so young." Just then I hear the sound that send shivers through my spine: It's the buzz of Derrick's heart monitor. Several nurses rush past me. I hear all sorts of commotion going on inside of the room, but I cannot make myself go back. My body seems to be frozen in place. One of the nurses walks out of the room.

"Is he ok?" I ask. Even though I know the answer.

She pauses for a moment, looks directly into my eyes and says, "No, he's gone. I'm sorry."

"Noooooooooooo!!!!!!!!!" I jump up and run back into the room. A nurse is about to pull the sheet over him. "No! I'll do that." She walks out of the room and I walk towards the bed. I pull the chair up near the bed and lay my head on Derrick's chest. "Oh, Derrick." I whisper through the tears. I run my hands over his body. I feel every bone and remember how he used to feel. The pain inside of me is intense. It's heavy. I feel so helpless and empty. A part of me has died.

Everything that I've gone through up to this moment seems trivial. Derrick is gone and all that is left are memories. In this moment I realize how incredibly precious life is and how every moment that we live and breathe is a blessing. I tell myself that I will make the most of mine.

CHAPTER 47

The funeral was touching. Not long, drawn out and depressing like most funerals, but rather a loving homecoming. A few relatives and friends said some comforting words and the minister completed the ceremony with an uplifting eulogy. The family decided that it would be a closed casket service because of the damage that the cancer had done. It was decided that people should remember Derrick prior to his death and that seeing his frail body would only make the pain worse. A nice 8x10 photo sat on top of the casket. Derrick was so incredibly handsome and as painful as it was seeing him on his death bed, I'm glad that I had the chance to see him before he died. I feel as if we finally closed the chapter on our relationship. There isn't much conversation taking place between my sisterfriends and I as we pulled up to my place. I suppose we are all trying to let everything sink in. I put my purse down on my end table and sit on my ottoman.

"Whew! What a day. I still cannot believe that Derrick is dead," Naomi says.

"I know what you mean," Renee says. "I mean it just doesn't seem real. I'll be the first to admit that I despised Derrick for hurting Nat, but I never wished his death."

"I'm there with you Renee. I felt the same way. It's just too much, not to mention Lela showing up. God, she has a lot of nerve." Taylor runs her fingers through her hair and starts to massage her temples as if a headache is coming on.

"She's a trip!" Renee says.

"Nat, what did she say to you?" I give no response. "Nat?"

"Uh, huh?" I say almost in a daze.

"Nat, you ok?" Naomi asks.

"Yeah, I'm ok." I get up and walk into the kitchen. My friends follow me. I grab a bottle of wine from the fridge and pour us each a glass.

"So, what did she say? Naomi asks again.

"Who?" I ask.

"Lela."

"Oh, she just wanted to apologize again and asked if there was ever a chance of us being friends again."

"No she didn't!" Taylor snaps.

"That heifer is glad that you are not me because she wouldn't have been able to say shit to me. How dare her. Friends? I don't think so." Renee is really pissed off.

"Listen you guys, I'm over it. It's done. Let's not re-hash everything. Lela has to deal with this matter in her own way. If that means apologizing to me, oh well. But I can honestly say that I am not wasting another moment thinking about the past. Derrick's death taught me that. I am going to focus on today and the good things that are a part of my life."

"So, what did you say to her?" Taylor asks.

"I told Lela that I forgave her but I didn't know if we could ever be friends again," I take a sip of wine, "I explained to her that I didn't hold any grudges towards her and that I wished her the best. We hugged and that was it."

"Man Nat, you're bigger than me. I don't know if I could forgive a friend for doing that to me," Naomi says.

"You could. After pondering long and hard about the situation, you'd realize that it would be a waste of energy to carry around with you every day of your life. And sooner or later you'd ask God to take it away from you. That's exactly what I did. I released it all to God. And you know what? I'm a better person because of it." Everyone nods in unison as if they really got it. "That's why it is so important to love and cherish those close to you. Think before you do something cruel to a friend. Ask yourself, is it worth it? Lela, didn't think and she lost not only one friend, but four."

"I know that's right." Renee says.

"I love you guys," I say out loud. Everyone smiles and we embrace.

"We love you too," they each say as tears roll down each of our faces. I think that we're each sad that Lela isn't a part of our sisterhood, but we also realize that this tragedy has made our love and friendship stronger.

"Let's go get something to eat!" Taylor says.

"Girl, you are always hungry." I say while nudging her lightly.

"This is true, now let's go."

We grab our purses and head to the car.

2 YEARS LATER

The warmth of the sun beams through my bay window and feels good against my skin. I'm standing in my kitchen slicing some fresh tomatoes. I've decided to try this eggplant dish that I saw on the "Better Homes & Gardens" show. Since I've been home for the last few weeks, I've been catching up on my culinary skills. Now, everyone stops by after work because they know that I've watched some cooking show and have whipped up something grand. Life has been so good. I can't believe what a difference two years has made. My news career is going great. Who would have guessed that I would be in line to anchor the early evening newscast? Just yesterday I was a scared college graduate trying to get my feet wet and today one of the most popular news anchors in Vegas. Wow! God is good. So much has happened since Derrick's death. I have really worked hard at living each day to its fullest. I didn't want to take anything or anyone for granted. Now when I wake up, I relish at being able to see the incredible works of God. Life is a gift, and it took a death to really put it in perspective.

And now an update on my life. Day and her family moved to Las Vegas last year. I am so happy that my sister and I are finally in the same city again. We have been having a blast. My sisterfriends are all doing fabu. Naomi's financial planning business is going great. Her clientele has really picked up since she started doing television ads. My station put together some really nice spots for her company. Naomi and her sweetie John got married last year and are doing quite well. Taylor is still teaching. She still hasn't found anyone special, but you know that she's making her rounds and still shoutin' at church on Sundays. That's Taylor. Renee is married. Believe it or not she married a guy that she met on the Internet. I know, I couldn't believe it either, but James is absolutely wonderful. We all thought that she and Tony were going to hook up, but he got caught with a white girl. Chile, that's a whole different book. Lela and I have spoken a few times and with each conversation a layer of tension has been let down. I still don't think that we'll ever be as close as we were, but we are attempting to rebuild our friendship.

Oh, before I forget, Derrick left me a large sum of money in his will. Most people didn't know that he was a brilliant investor. Anyway, I really didn't need the money, but I wanted to put it to good use. So, I started an education fund for Antonio. Remember him? Yeah, he's still around. He completed the boot camp and is preparing to attend Grambling State University in the fall. He has become such a nice young man. I also put the down payment on a home for him and his family. Antonio's mother is finally clean and sober. She works as a counselor at the local women's shelter. I know that Derrick would be pleased with what I've done with his gift. I took the rest of the money and started two more education funds. I'll fill you in on that later.

I feel some strong arms wrap around me and then a soft kiss on my neck.

"Mmmmm, what are you smiling about?"

"Oh, I was just thinking about how incredibly blessed I am. We are."

"I'm feeling you." He pauses just long enough to turn me towards him. "How are you and my little ones doing this morning?"

"We're doing just fine."

Miles takes his hand and starts to rub my stomach gently as he's done every morning since we found out that we were pregnant. He gets on his knees and begins to talk, "Good morning Daddy's babies! It's a beautiful day. Watcha doing in there?" The babies start moving and the sensation makes me laugh.

"Oh, honey stop! You know that they get excited when they hear your voice."

Proudly, he says, "Yes, they do know their Daddy." We both laugh.

Well, you've probably guessed by now that Miles and I tied the knot. Yep, last year on Valentine's Day. Happiness in an understatement. I am so filled with joy. I have never known love like this. It is incredible waking up next to someone who loves you unconditionally. Miles is everything that I dreamed of and more. This man moves me. He caresses my soul. He is my air. He was so patient with me, and once I really let my guard down and let him in, all I can say is that it's been heaven ever since.

Miles is still on his knees. I begin to rub his head.

"You hungry honey?" I ask.

"Uh, huh," he says while letting his hands slip beneath my gown. Even though my stomach is taking up half of the kitchen we still are able to have the most loving hugs. He still touches me with a gentleness that only he knows.

"Natalie?" He stands and holds me.

"Yes baby," I softly pant.

""You are my world."

"And you are mine." We kiss softly. I feel warmth between my thighs.

"Honey?" I whisper.

"Yeah," he says not really paying attention to a word I'm saying.

"It's time."

"Uh, huh." He kisses my neck.

"Honey, my water just broke." Miles jumps back and begins running around the kitchen like a mad man.

"Do you have your bag ready? Yeah, it's in the car? What about your book? The music?" He's just having a conversation with himself.

I laugh to myself at how frantic he's become. I put the tomatoes in the fridge, wipe off the counter and head upstairs. Of course Miles is still running around. I go into the bathroom and turn on the shower. I feel myself getting nervous and anxious. I am really going to have some babies in a few hours. This is really too much. I start to breathe slowly as I step into the shower. The warm water helps to keep me calm. I hear Miles come into the bathroom.

"Baby, you ok?" He asks in a nervous tone.

"I'm fine honey. Come here please." He walks to the shower door and opens it. "Come in with me." I say. Miles undresses quickly and steps inside of the shower. We just hold each other and begin to cry. I guess we're both feeling as if our lives have come full circle.

"Do you realize that this is the last time that I'm going to see you like this for awhile?"

"For awhile?" I laugh. "Babe, you're getting a two for one deal."

"Oh, I think we can work on another in about two years." He laughs and pulls me closer.

"We'll see. We'll see." I say

'You scared?" Miles asks.

"A little bit, but I can't wait to see them! I know that they're going to be precious."

"Just like their Mommy."

"I love you Miles."

"I love you more."

We finish showering and head to the hospital. I grab my cell and call my sister. She is so excited that she's finally going to be an aunt. Day tells me that she'll meet us at the hospital and she'll call my sisterfriends. Of course, they all beat us to the hospital and are standing outside waiting for us when we arrive. Miles and I just die laughing when we see them all standing there. It's like our own welcoming committee.

Fourteen hours, 20 minutes and 10 seconds later, we welcome Micah and Micayla Grey into this wonderful world. Let me tell you, having twins is no joke. But I wouldn't trade the experience for the world. I finally have my own family. I'm really blessed.

So, that's my story! Pretty exciting, huh? You never know what life has in store for you or what path you'll take. I've learned a few things along the way. Put God first, surround yourself with family and "true" friends, and most important: Give love and it will be given to you. Got it? Good!

Special Thanks: It seems as if it has taken me forever to get my baby published, but it's finally here and I am grateful. My life is a blessing and I have been fortunate to have a wonderful circle of sisterfriends. I can't imagine my life without you. Though many of us live in different cities and may not talk as often as we'd like to…know that I love you and you've touched my life in a special way. I will attempt to honor each of you by naming you in the order in which you entered my life: Renee Turner, Tanya Evans, Tracy Story, Kyra Lay, Demetrious Gibson, Lula Lee, Carla Matthews Patrick, Terri Giles, Zannavia Willpitz, Friday Williams, Deborah Buffett, Tressa Fernandez, Wendy Shelton, Deborah McCall, Karen Lewis, Murphy Hickerson, TTT(DST), Veronica Swett, Johnetta Walton, Corlette Williams, Ruby Smith, Verlon Malone, Elyse Adler, Marian Christmon, Stella Thompson, Doretha Ramsey, Christyna Ferrell, Sisters of the Soul, Brooke Myatt, Alina Smith, and Sandra Johnson. Tasneem (I couldn't have done this without you). My mentors: Eva Simmons, Deborah Jackson, Barbara Coleman, Belinda Thompson, Carolyn Shelton, Phyllis Greer, and Faye Duncan-Daniels. The Porter Family. The Brooks Family. My sisters: Debbra Brooks and Valerie Wright. My brother: Reginald Brooks. My god sister: Gwynne Barnes. Timmy Jackson (You're a wonderful artist). The West Las Vegas Library and the Nashville Public Library. Last, but certainly not least…the love of my life. Scott, thank you for loving me mind, body and soul...I adore you!

Special Note: My soul still aches when I think of the lives affected by Hurricane Katrina. When this disaster first struck New Orleans, I like so many gave money and donating items to help those in need. Recently, I watched Spike Lee's documentary *When the Levees Broke,* and was left completely numb. I sat in bed and asked myself what more could I do. My first thought was that I didn't have a lot of money or resources, but then I thought about my novel. I knew I was getting ready to self publish and decided that I needed to do something more. I couldn't rest on the thoughts of what I couldn't do. I had to focus on what I could do. Therefore, I am donating a dollar from every book sold to assist the families that were affected by Hurricane Katrina. I (We) cannot forget our sisters and brothers.

Book Club or Roundtable Discussion Questions:

1. *Is it possible to love two people at the same time?*
2. *Have you ever loved two people at the same time? Was the love equal?*
3. *Discuss the difference between love and lust. Why do women tend to get it wrong most of the time?*
4. *If you had the opportunity to rekindle an affair with your first love, would you do it? What if you knew it would last?*
5. *Why was it so difficult for Natalie to get Derrick out of her system?*
6. *Was Derrick a bad guy?*
7. *What would you do if you found your best friend in bed with the man you loved?*
8. *Could the friendship be saved?*
9. *Do you have to go through a terrible storm before your Prince Charming arrives?*
10. *How do you recognize Prince Charming?*
11. *Are you generally attracted to men like Derrick or men like Miles?*
12. *What is the overall lesson in this novel?*

Dear Reader,

Thank you for reading Torn Between 2 Brothas. I hope that you enjoyed it and will share it with others. If you have a story that you'd like to share about loving two people or just want to drop me a line, please e-mail me at: lindaporter@hotmail.com

Thanks for your support!

SmH